With God's Help:
Building the McFarlin Church

Author;
Beverly I. Sanders

Illustrations by Patty Castle
Copyright 1998

With God's Help: Building the McFarlin Church, Copyright © 1998 Beverly I. Sanders

All rights reserved.

ISBN: 9798876784803

Dedication

Robert M. and Ida B. McFarlin were living in Norman, Oklahoma in 1893 when their infant son, Robert Boger, died of typhoid fever. Years later, after making a fortune in the oil business, Robert and Ida McFarlin gave a church to the community in memory of their son.

Others whose names are not so well known are the ministers E. R. Welch, C. S. Walker, W. L. Broome, and L. S. Barton. All contributed to the effort to build a new church in different ways.

Gilbert H. Smith, an ordained Methodist Episcopal South minister and sociology professor at the University of Oklahoma, came to Norman in 1914. He soon developed a vision of a University-Community church serving both the community and the students. He and the students in his University Bible Class worked for many years before finally seeing that vision realized through the generosity of the McFarlins.

This book is dedicated to the memory of all these people with thanks to God that He saw fit to place them here at the time they were so needed to make possible the building of McFarlin Memorial United Methodist Church.

Foreword

During the years between 1890 and 1924 significant events and a group of people with a vision came together in the small university town of Norman, Oklahoma. Some of the events involved the death of a child, the discovery of oil, and the rise to wealth of a humble man. The people included a professor with a driving vision of a community and university church, the Methodist Episcopal South ministers who shared that vision and worked for it, and a couple who gave generously from their wealth to make it come true. Under God's guiding hand, these events and people brought about the building of the McFarlin Memorial Methodist Church, a glorious house of worship which is now approaching its hundredth year of service to the university students and the community. It is this anniversary that inspired the republishing of this book.

This is a work of historical fiction. That is, the main characters and events, while fictional, are set against a background of events and persons that are as historically authentic as available information can make them.

Professor G. H. Smith; the Reverends Welch, Walker, Broome and Barton; Bishop Mouzon; and above all, Robert and Ida McFarlin, are real persons and were among those who were inspired to bring about the building of this great church.

The Cunninghams and their friends and neighbors are all fictional. I would not want their story to overshadow the real story, which is the building of this church. Their story was invented to represent the ways that McFarlin Memorial United Methodist Church touched and blessed lives even before it was built.

The church's dedication plaque says, "This House of Worship is built for the Youth of Oklahoma and the People of Norman, and whomsoever may find it in his heart to worship here." McFarlin Memorial United Methodist Church continues to faithfully fulfill that mission. It is important that each new generation know how the hand of God was at work in the events surrounding the construction of this building.

Contents

Acknowledgments	i
Chapter 1	1
Chapter 2	7
Chapter 3	12
Chapter 4	22
Chapter 5	27
Chapter 6	32
Chapter 7	39
Chapter 8	45
Chapter 9	51
Chapter 10	57
Chapter 11	64
Chapter 12	68
Chapter 13	73
Chapter 14	82
Chapter 15	89
Chapter 16	97

Acknowledgments

Many people have contributed to the completion of this book. My husband, Joe Sanders, spent many hours helping me research old newspapers, and then faithfully proofread and critiqued every chapter as it came from my computer. Nina Zapffe and my daughter Janice Mullan contributed greatly to the correctness of grammar, form, and spelling. Betsy Pain, Kathy Mash, the 75thAnniversary Committee, and the Two in One Sunday School class have given constant support and encouragement to the project. Special thanks to Judi Knapp for her work to assure professional and technical correctness. Patty Castle so thoroughly researched her drawings that she has added points of correctness to the manuscript material. Her magnificent drawings capture the characters of the story to perfection.

Historical information for this project has come from: Numerous articles from The *Norman Transcript*. Norman, OK: 1917-1924

Smith, Rev. Gilbert H. *Letter to Rev. Don Schooler.*
26 January 1965. Copy at McFarlin Memorial United Methodist Church, Norman, OK.

Tyson, Carl N., James H. Thomas, and Odie B. Faulk.
The McMan: *The Lives of Robert M. McFarlin and James A. Chapman.*
Norman, OK: University of Oklahoma Press, 1977.

With God's Help: Building the McFarlin Church is a historical work of fiction. Names, characters, places and incidents are based on real events but are products of the author's imagination for the purpose of telling the story and the events surrounding it. Any resemblance to actual events, locales, or persons, living or dead, is meant only in the best presentation of the real events, places, and people involved.

Chapter 1

Callie Sue crawled through the maze of chair and table legs under the dining room table.

"Slap! Slap!" went the dust cloth, making an angry sound against the already shining wood. Callie's frowning reflection looked back at her as she continued to creep along, rubbing each leg and rung.

"I can't see what difference it makes," she grumbled. "Dust, dust, dust every day! No matter how much dust I wipe away, there's always more before I finish."

There was a lot of truth in Callie Sue's thinking. It seemed like it never failed. If Mama made Callie Sue do her dusting early in the morning, it wasn't any time before Mr. Simmons came rumbling by in the big dairy wagon pulled by his team of gray work horses, hauling his milk to Norman. The summer heat had dried the road to a fine powder, and great clouds would rise behind the hooves and wheels. Callie Sue could only watch as the clouds came floating lazily toward the house with its open windows and doors. Sometimes she wanted to run around and close everything quickly before the gray mist came in. Of course, you couldn't do that! It was July, and the summer heat was fierce.

Every night Mama and Papa said to each other at the dinner table, "Seems like this is just about the hottest and driest summer I ever remember here in Oklahoma!"

Callie didn't know if it was any hotter and dryer this summer of 1919 than any other year, but it was hot all right. It was certainly too hot to think of closing the doors and windows to keep the dust out. Even if you tried, you'd be opening and closing windows all day long. For, after Mr. Simmons, there might be a load of field hands headed out to the Johnson's to hoe the cotton or to the Meyers' to pick green beans. So, the traffic went all day long, up and down the dusty road in front of their house.

One day last summer Mama had let Callie Sue wait till after noon to dust, and she had thought, "Now it will still be clean tomorrow, and I won't have to do it then."

She hadn't even finished when along came Mr. Simmons returning from Norman with his now empty milk cans rattling and clanking as the horses trotted down the road, eager to get home to their corral, their feed, and rest. She had watched in despair as the inevitable clouds rolled toward her freshly dusted furniture.

Sometimes Callie wished their house was way back on the far corner of their farm, far away from the road with all its dust and dirt. That wouldn't be much fun though. There were many times when a day's only excitement was to watch the wagons, buggies, and carriages as people went by. There was certainly little enough excitement for a nine year-old living on a farm a mile outside the little town of Norman. Callie always waved if she recognized their neighbors, especially when she saw any of her friends from school. Neighbors used to stop for a minute, although that didn't happen much anymore. There were more and more automobiles in town, but they didn't often come out this far. So, if she heard the chugging and sputtering of a motor, Callie would hurry to see the bright, shiny motor car go bouncing by.

Then there were the funeral processions that went slowly and mournfully into the cemetery across the road. Sometimes she ran and hid behind a tree or gravestone to count the carriages and automobiles as they went in, knowing that if there were many, the person must have been very important in town.

"I wonder," she sometimes thought, "how many cars and buggies would be in my procession if I died, or in Jeremy's if he had died?"

Callie always stopped then, closed her eyes and shook her head as if to rid herself of those thoughts. She didn't want them there, but sometimes they just slipped in when she wasn't ready for them.

Now Callie Sue gave her head a good shake, took one more swipe at a table leg, and crawled out. She ran outside to put her dust rag on the clothesline to air out and stuck her head back inside the door.

"Mama," she called, "I'm all finished dusting. I'm going to go play for a little while."

She let the screen door slam and dashed off, eager to be away. She felt just a little guilty. What if Mama had wanted to call her back to snap the beans for dinner, or to stir the gravy, or slice the bread? Callie knew that she really had closed that door so

With God's Help: Building the McFarlin Church

quickly just so she could truthfully say, "I didn't hear you call."

It wasn't that she was lazy, or wanted to shirk her chores. It was just that it always seemed so solemn and sad around the house now. Mama didn't smile much anymore, and Callie couldn't remember when she last heard her mother singing as she went about her work. It had also been months since Beauty and Blaze had been hitched to the buckboard to take the family into Norman for shopping. Mostly, Papa just picked up a few supplies when he went in with the wagon, while Mama and Callie stayed home with Jeremy.

Papa used to go whistling out to the fields, talking and joking with the big gray work horses, encouraging them with "Step lively there, Dan! Good girl, Daisy!" Now it was just "Giddap there!" or "Whoa!"

Callie couldn't remember when Papa had last pulled her pigtails or teased about his "freckle-nosed Susie." Every now and then she had to escape from all the quiet sadness.

Her refuge, her destination now, was the peaceful cemetery just across the road. Once inside the fence, she wandered along letting her hand caress the smooth coolness of first one stone and then another. She paused by one that was formed like a small tree trunk and trailed her fingers along its stone bark. Nearby a stone dove perched peacefully atop a light gray stone. She looked around for a cool spot and decided on the shade of a small cedar tree. She flopped on her stomach in the cool grass and, chin on hands, studied a large black ant busily picking its way among the blades of grass. It crawled up onto a small bluish gray marker, took a diagonal path across it, and was soon lost in the grass on the other side.

Callie Sue finds refuge in the cemetery.

Callie Sue looked at the marker and traced her fingers over the words carved into the stone, **Robert Boger, Son of R. M. & I. M. McFarlin. Died July 28, 1893, Aged 1Yr. 7M's. 10 D's**.

"Just over 19 months," she thought, "such a little boy!"

She rolled over, put her head back, and closed her eyes. "Were you someone's brother?" she wondered. Her thoughts drifted back to the gloomy house she had just escaped. "Did you have a sister to miss you and cry for you?"

Callie made herself sit up and she opened her eyes. "Your brother did not die!" she told herself sternly. "Quit thinking like that!"

"Maybe so," her mind argued, but it's just as if he had. He never says a word to you. He never takes you out to see lizards and turtles and rabbits like he did before. It's like Mama and Daddy are in mourning, they seem so sad all the time. Whether he's dead or not, you've lost your brother."

Tears started to find their way down her cheeks, and she closed her eyes again. The place was so quiet and peaceful she felt somehow soothed. Finally, she dried her tears and lay there remembering what it had been like before. The shade from her little tree was almost gone now, so it must be nearly noon. She knew she had to go back, but she would wait as long as she could before returning to the house to sit down to another sad and gloomy dinner.

Chapter 2

Callie Sue swung her feet under her chair, stared at the shining wood under the table, and waited for the food to be passed.
"Look, Jeremy," said Mama, "Your favorite summer meal! Corn on the cob, fried okra, fried chicken, and sliced tomatoes! Here's a drumstick especially for you!"
Callie held her breath. Maybe this time Jeremy would laugh like he used to and tell Mama she was the best cook in all of Oklahoma. But, no, nothing had changed. Jeremy took a chicken wing and a few pieces of okra on his plate, along with a slice of fresh red tomato. Then he sat and stared at the plate. With his fork, he moved the food around from here to there, taking only a few small bites. Mama sighed, shook her head, and looked like she would start to cry again. She did that so much these days!
Callie hooked her toes behind the rung of her chair, not caring that she was messing up her careful dusting job. Mama used to inspect her dusting every morning saying, "I'm not going to ask the Lord to bless food set out on a dusty table." Now she wondered if Mama had even looked. "Jeremy, please pass the bread," said Callie. Now he would have to at least look at her! Jeremy grunted something she could not understand and pushed the plate across the

table at her. Well, if he wouldn't talk, she could at least try to get some response from the rest of her family! "Guess what, Mama. I saw Miss Miller go by in her buggy this morning. Looked like she was going down to the schoolhouse. I wonder why a teacher has to go to the school even in the middle of summer?"

Of course, Callie knew there was always work for a teacher, but Mama had always liked Miss Miller, and maybe thinking about her would at least catch Mama's interest for a little while.

It seemed as if Mama hadn't even heard her. "Jeremy, you need some butter for your corn. I churned the butter just today."

Jeremy grunted again, shook his head, and shoved the butter aside.

Callie took a deep breath and tried again. "Papa, there was a really big funeral yesterday. I counted at least thirty…" Seeing the look on Mama and Papa's faces, Callie Sue stopped mid-sentence. That had been a mistake! Thinking about funerals just reminded them how close they had come to having a funeral for Jeremy.

Callie gave up, and began mechanically eating the delicious food. It could just as well have been sawdust. At last, the silent meal was finished. Mama and Papa both rushed around the table as Jeremy made a motion to move his chair. Papa carefully pulled out the chair as Mama got the crutches. They each took hold of one of Jeremy's arms.

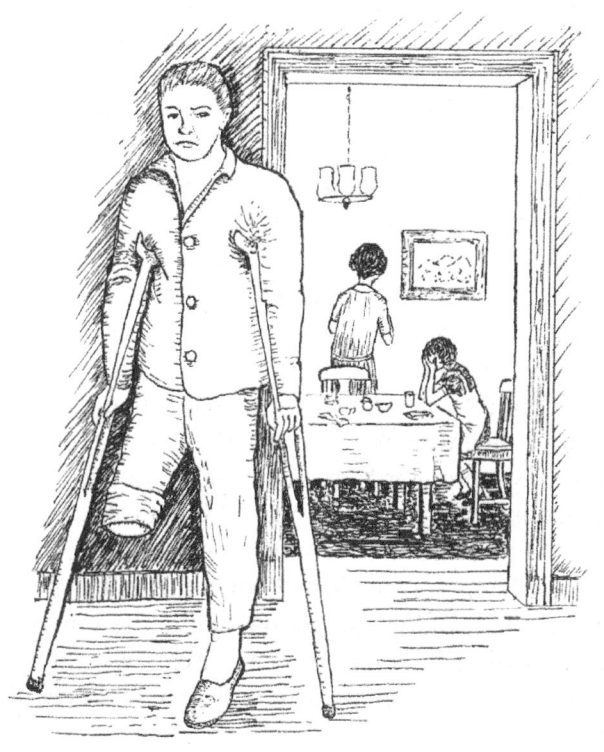

Jeremy leaves the family table.

"Let me alone! I can do it!" Jeremy's face twisted in anger, and his whistling, wheezy voice came out in the closest thing to a shout he could manage. Callie cringed, closed her eyes and covered her ears. She didn't want to see or hear as Jeremy struggled to raise himself on his one leg, or as he worked with the crutches to get them firmly under his arms. The exertion would cause him to breathe so heavily, with the air whistling in and out of his lungs, that soon he would break into a fit of coughing. Mama would stand by twisting her hands while he gasped and struggled for each breath. It would finally end with Jeremy on his crutches pulling himself down the hall to his room, his stump of a leg swinging uselessly. Then Papa would slam the door on his way out to the barn, and Mama would shut herself in her room. Later she would reappear, her hair freshly combed, but her eyes red and moist with tears. Callie had seen it so often that she knew the scene by heart. This time, however, there was something new.

Jeremy uttered a string of words that Callie had never heard before. From her mother's gasp she knew they were words that would never have been allowed in this house. She heard Mama sob and hurry off to her room, then the clump, shuffle, and swish as Jeremy went slowly down the hall. Callie felt that she could not stand to listen to the sounds, and she still had her hands over her ears when Papa slammed the door on his way to the barn. When all was quiet, Callie Sue quickly cleared the table and took the dishes to the kitchen. She filled the dishpan with hot water from the kettle, whipped up some suds, and hurriedly washed and rinsed the dishes. She didn't even worry about the salty tears falling down her cheeks and into the dishwater.

Finally finished, she called out, "Mama, I'm going outside!"

Knowing there would be no answer, she dashed out the door, up the driveway, and through the fence. Once inside the cool cemetery, she ran blindly to the spot near the little cedar. She threw herself on the ground and pounded it with her fists. "I hate it! I hate THE WAR!" she screamed. "Nothing will ever be right again! Why did it have to happen?"

The tears came freely with no one near and no reason to hide them. Callie bawled loudly and openly until there were no more tears. She breathed deeply and thought, "We all expected Jeremy to get better, but he hasn't, and it's been over seven months now since he came home. No, that's not right. Jeremy didn't come home. Some stranger came home. He just looked like Jeremy!"

Chapter 3

Exhausted from her tears; Callie Sue rolled over and ran her fingers over the grave marker.

"Little Robert Boger Mcfarlin, what happened to you? Were you killed in an accident? Or drowned in the creek? I know you didn't go off to war. Maybe you caught some terrible disease. There probably weren't many doctors here in 1893, and they probably didn't even know as much then as they do now."

Callie had once thought that doctors could fix anything that was wrong with you, but she had found out how wrong that was. When they brought Jeremy home there were many times the doctor had felt just as helpless as Mama and Papa. He finally told them, "Your son is alive. We doctors have done all we can. The rest will take something more."

If Robert Boger McFarlin had grown up, would he have marched off to the war too?

THE WAR! That was the way the grownups always said it. Without even seeing it, you felt as if it were all capital letters. That was how Callie thought of it now.

It had all been so confusing. It must have started before Callie Sue was old enough to remember. About two years ago she began to notice that adult conversations always got around to, "Would the United States join in the war?" They

With God's Help: Building the McFarlin Church

talked in hushed voices whenever the newspaper came out. Maybe they had thought that if they didn't say it out loud, it would not be true. Callie heard them and knew they were worried. She had felt a gnawing fear in her stomach every time she heard the whispers about, "The Germans--The Kaiser--Zeppelin raids--The Huns are using poison gas--U-boats in the Atlantic." She hadn't understood what it meant, but somehow had known it was bad... worse than anything she had ever known in her lifetime.

She hadn't understood what the older boys found so exciting about it all. Seth Bridges from down the road came by often during that spring of 1917. He and Jeremy had been in school together ever since they started first grade. They couldn't understand why their parents said they couldn't enlist until they had finished high school in May. Other boys came by and there were long, loud arguments about "Isolationism" or "American responsibility to the world." She had often heard some of the boys say, "Just wait till the United States gets over there. We'll show them how to end this thing!"

And the Norman boys had especially liked to brag, "Ten Oklahomans can lick a hundred Germans any time!" Then it happened. The newspaper headlines proclaimed in huge black letters, "U.S. DECLARES WAR!"

Right after graduation the young men hurried to enlist and get into uniform. Then they went all around town, swaggering and singing "Over There."

No one ever said "Over Where?" If you were old enough, you knew where, and if you didn't know, then you knew better than to ask.

Jeremy had looked handsome in his uniform. Callie could hardly believe this young man was the brother she had always known. Was this the same straw-hatted boy who had always had time to take her to town with him or into the fields to show her the difference between toads and frogs, or which snakes were good and which were poisonous? Callie had felt shy as he stood straight and tall and gave a ragged version of a salute. Jeremy had been happy and excited, but Mama and Papa had worn sad, worried looks that wouldn't go away.

Then the young men marched away! Right down Main Street to the train depot and onto the train bound for Camp Travis, Texas! Mothers, fathers, families, and neighbors waved and cheered, even though their throats were hoarse and tight with tears. The boys on the train shouted back, "We'll finish this and be back in no time!"

Then the train pulled away, taking Norman's fine, strong, and healthy young men with it.

Months passed, and everyone anxiously followed the progress of the war. When one set of parents got a letter from their son, they hurried to share with the neighbors, for most of the Norman boys were in the same outfit. At first the letters were about the training. It was tough, but nothing a hardy farm boy from Oklahoma couldn't handle! Then, after training, there came the shipping out!

With God's Help: Building the McFarlin Church

Some of the Norman boys seemed surprised that even soldiers got seasick, but in many letters home they grudgingly admitted to having a rather rough crossing.

Then they talked about what a welcome they received in England. They had arrived to enthusiastic cheers. The English had served them coffee and doughnuts and treated them like family.

Then the letters home came less often. Newspapers told of U.S. forces in one battle and then another. Parents read the headlines and looked more worried than ever. The U.S. forces didn't seem to be mopping it up quite as quickly as predicted! Even when letters came, it was just, "We were in a bit of a fight, but we came out O.K." In truth, so little reassurance was no reassurance at all.

The months had dragged on.

Without Jeremy's help, Papa wasn't able to farm all the fields, and planted only those closest to the house. Anxiously, Papa and Mama read every word in every newspaper, hoping for, and yet dreading news of Jeremy's unit. Even Callie Sue had read the headlines, "U.S. Forces Driven Back," and "Germans Use Poison Gas."

At first Callie had asked "What is poison gas?," or "Are we winning? Will Jeremy be home soon?" Mama had gotten so upset, though, that Callie soon quit asking.

Then the official letters started to come. The first letter went to the Perkins from south of town, near Noble. Their son had been wounded in action, and was in the hospital. Then the Rivers' son,

15

William, had been killed in action and arrangements had to be made to ship his personal belongings home. Then one day Mrs. Bridges came hurrying in with her letter! A shell had exploded right beside Seth. He had been badly injured, but would live. He had lost his left hand and eye. Callie wondered if her parents felt as she did, a sense of guilt, yet relief, each time that it was not Jeremy.

But then it happened! Jeremy was wounded, and was taken to a military hospital in England. The family was to be notified when he was returned to the states. Mama and Papa nearly went crazy with wondering, "How bad? What happened?" No more information had come, and there were no letters from Jeremy.

Finally, the news came, Jeremy was in the states and could come home, but he would need someone to escort him. The Bridges had received the same news about Seth. The families scraped together the money, and Mama and Mrs. Bridges left on the long train trip to bring their son's home. Callie felt like she couldn't stand her excitement as she waited out the days for her brother to come home.

It was during this time that the news came: On November 11, 1918, the armistice was signed. The town was filled with people cheering and celebrating. Callie Sue felt like shouting at them all, "How can you celebrate? My brother is hurt and, in a hospital somewhere!" She knew, though, that hers was not the only family for whom the armistice had come too late.

With God's Help: Building the McFarlin Church

When the train pulled in, Papa climbed aboard and he and the conductor carefully lifted Jeremy down onto the station platform. Callie Sue thought, "This can't be Jeremy!" He was so thin! His skin looked gray and dry, and worst of all, below his knee there was a flat empty pants leg. This had to be a nightmare; surely, she would wake up soon!

Seth Bridges and his mother were next off the train. As Seth was helped down the steps, they could see that his head and left arm were covered with bandages. He was badly wounded, but Callie Sue couldn't help a fleeting instant of jealousy. He was on his own feet!

The nightmare hadn't gone away. The days and weeks dragged on. The government provided medical help for the wounded veterans, and they had seen doctor after doctor.

The poison gas left Jeremy's lungs damaged, and when he breathed, the gasp and rattle echoed throughout the house. Jeremy had arrived home in the midst of the influenza epidemic, and the county was under quarantine during October and November. The doctors admitted that treatment for poison gas injuries was new to them, and they did not know what to expect. So, catching the flu could be especially disastrous for Jeremy in his weakened condition. The doctors speculated that once the danger of influenza was gone, fresh air and exercise might help. When they tried to talk to Jeremy about a program of therapy, however, he only became more surly, turned his back, and told everybody to leave him alone.

With God's Help: Building the McFarlin Church

The doctors talked about the wonderful improvements in artificial limbs, and how Jeremy could be fitted in a few more months when the stump below his knee was better healed. Jeremy just growled that they wouldn't catch him clumping around with a wooden leg, and the subject was closed.

The family had always attended church regularly at the little Methodist Episcopal Church South in Norman, but since Jeremy had been home Mama and Papa had been so busy with him that it seemed that no one even thought about church. One day, however, as Christmas approached, Mama hesitantly suggested that they help Jeremy into the buckboard so they all could attend the church service.

Jeremy just growled, "I don't want anything to do with the God that let this happen."

Christmas came. It should have been a joyful celebration with the war over and Jeremy home. It wasn't; it was more like going to a funeral. No one felt like shopping or singing carols. Jeremy was home, but he wasn't Jeremy. Staying home had become a habit, and none of the family went to church or anywhere else much. Brother Walker, the minister from their church, tried to visit, but Jeremy was so rude that he soon gave it up. Now seven months had passed and nothing had changed. If anything, it was even worse. Until today, Jeremy had never cursed in their home before.

With God's Help: Building the McFarlin Church

Callie Sue meets Mr. Groggins.

Now swishing and shuffling sounds broke through Callie Sue's sad thoughts. They were coming closer, and she opened her eyes to see what could be making the sounds. She sat up quickly and wiped her hands across her tear stained face. An elderly man in overalls was limping slowly along the path. He carried a small hand scythe and stopped every few steps to stoop and cut bunches of grass that had grown tall. He stopped in surprise when he saw her.
"Well, I declare! It's not often I run into a young lady resting on the grass here in the cemetery.

You all right, Sis?" Callie Sue nodded her head as she scrubbed at her eyes.

The old man nodded back and carefully didn't notice her red eyes and streaked face.

"Sam Groggins is my name. I live just a bit down the road there," he said pointing off to the east.

He studied Callie Sue carefully. "You're one of the Cunninghams, aren't you?"

Callie Sue nodded again. "I'm Callie Sue Cunningham. I'm the youngest," she said in a small voice.

Taking a better look at Mr. Groggins. She realized that he was one of their neighbors, and that they used to see him and his wife every Sunday in church. Of course, that was before Jeremy came home.

"I do a bit of trimming and weeding around here," Mr. Groggins said, gesturing to indicate the neatly kept graves. "I try to keep the place looking nice. They pay me a little, but I like being out in the sun and air anyway. Sure, miss being able to keep up the farm anymore." He rubbed his right hand and straightened his back with a grimace of pain. "Arthritis is sure slowing me down though!"

Callie Sue surveyed his work. "It looks very nice," she said politely.

She noticed then that it had begun to get dark and the shadow of the little cedar had grown long.

"Oh my! I have to go!" She knew she must go back, no matter how things were at home. "Bye, Mr. Groggins."

With God's Help: Building the McFarlin Church

"I'll come see you again, Robert," she whispered, patting the stone. "Now I have a place to go when things get too bad at the house."

At the fence, Callie paused to look back, wishing she didn't have to leave this quiet place. As she stood there, she heard a sound and saw a small farm wagon coming along the road. She waited to let it pass. It didn't pass, but turned in at their drive! That didn't often happen anymore. No one wanted to visit such a sad home! As she followed the wagon down the drive, she saw her mother at the screen door.

"Howdy, Mrs. Cunningham. Jeremy here?"

It was Seth Bridges, with a patch over his useless eye and no hand at the end of his left sleeve, but he sounded just as he always had when he had come looking for Jeremy!

Chapter 4

Seth put his good right hand on the wagon seat and jumped over the side, landing lightly on the ground. Callie couldn't help but be surprised at how skillfully he tied his team to the hitching rail with that one hand. They hadn't seen him since the day that he and Jeremy arrived on the train. Seth may have been on his own feet that day, but he had still been pale and sickly looking. Callie could hardly believe this tan, smiling young man was the same Seth.

"I figured it was about time I came around to visit with Jeremy," he said walking to the door. "I would've been by sooner, but Dad's been keeping me pretty busy helping with the haying and planting and all."

Callie Sue's mother just stared at Seth and silently opened the screen door. Callie followed him into the dimness of the room.

Seth paused a moment as he came in the door. "Seems to take a little while for my eye to adjust," he said.

Listening to his familiar voice, Callie wished that Jeremy could sound that way again. Jeremy and Seth had been together right up till Seth had been wounded and taken away to the hospital. That was also before their unit ran into the poison gas. Even so, the gas had been so fickle in the way it hung in pockets in low places, choking one soldier but missing the man next to him! Some of the men in the unit escaped, but many were injured. Why did Jeremy have to be one of the injured?

"It's not Seth's fault what happened to Jeremy!" Callie told herself sternly. "Besides, he was hurt awfully bad himself."

Callie's mother, recovering from her surprise, finally spoke. "Hello, Seth. It's good to see you! And looking so well!"

"I know I should have come by a long time ago. It's kept me pretty busy, relearning how to do everything that used to take both my hands, and adjusting to seeing with one eye, too." Seth shook his head, then smiled. "I'm not as much help to Dad as I used to be, but I'm getting better. Dad says I just have to use more brains now and less muscle."

Mama smiled sadly at that. "I wish... " she started, but then stopped and looked guiltily down the hall.

"I'll go get Jeremy," said Callie happily and hurried down the hall. "Jeremy, guess what. You've got company. Seth's here!"

Not a sound came from inside the room. Callie knocked and called again.

"Jeremy! Jeremy!" With a puzzled look she turned back to Seth and Mama, "Maybe he's asleep."

"Tell him to go away! I don't want to see him!"

Callie, standing right in front of the door, could barely hear the wheezing words, but from the

23

look on Seth's face she knew he had heard. He strode down the hall and opened the door without knocking.

"Now, Jeremy, you can't send me away! We've been pals too long. Here I've come to invite you on an outing and you talk to me like that! Pardon me, Mrs. Cunningham." He nodded to Callie and Mama, stepped into Jeremy's room, and shut the door.

Callie Sue and her mother looked at each other with some alarm.

"Should I go call Papa?" Callie asked.

"I don't think so. Not yet anyway," said Mama thoughtfully. "We've known Seth all his life, and I think we can trust him!"

They sat down nervously in the dim living room, resisting their need to stand with their ears pressed to the door. Mama twisted her hands nervously in her lap, then she picked up a newspaper and fanned herself. Callie picked up her rag doll and idly combed the golden yarn hair with her fingers. She rebraided the hair into two neat pigtails and fastened them with the gingham-checked ties.

The doll was forgotten and the newspaper fan stilled when loud voices came from behind the door. They couldn't hear the words, but the tones of anger were unmistakable. Seth spoke, paused, and spoke again, each time more angrily and louder. Then they would hear Jeremy's wheeze and whistle, even louder than his shout had been at lunch.

Seth invades Jeremy's room.

    Callie Sue and Mama exchanged worried looks as the argument went on. Then the coughing began, and still the angry voices continued. Would Jeremy hurt himself? Make his lungs even worse? Callie again wondered if she should go find Papa. Still Mama just listened, quiet and wide-eyed.
    Finally, the bedroom door jerked open. Seth came out and turned to face Jeremy.
    "Sunday morning!" he said, "Nine o'clock. Be ready!" One last muffled growl came from inside the room before Seth closed the door firmly and came back into the living room.

"I'm sorry about the shouting and all in your house, Mrs. Cunningham. I had a hard time convincing Jeremy. Sorry I can't stay to visit, but Dad's going to be needing my help. I'll be back Sunday morning, though. Jeremy's going with me to visit Professor Smith's University Bible Class." Callie and Mama simply stared at each other in speechless amazement. They moved to the door and watched silently as Seth untied his team. He put one foot on the step, took hold of the seat with his one good hand, and swung himself up into the wagon. The two of them were still standing at the door in surprise when he turned to wave before starting up the drive.

Chapter 5

Sunday morning dawned bright and sunny. Callie Sue, Mama, Papa, and Jeremy sat around the table at breakfast. Mama left her chair to get the coffee pot from the stove. She poured coffee for herself and Papa, then asked, "Coffee, Jeremy?"

His only answer was to hunch farther down into his chair and grunt. Mama, Papa, and Callie were all trying not to look out the front door and up the drive, trying not to look as if they were expecting someone. Mama went to the door, wiping her face with her apron.

"My! My! 8:30 in the morning and look how hot it is already. Looks like it's going to be another hot one today! Can you believe it's only 8:30?"

She gave Jeremy a hidden glance as she spoke. Jeremy, wearing an old bathrobe, just sat sullenly at the table. His eyes were fixed on his plate as he picked at the biscuit and sausage gravy that had grown cold long ago.

Mama and Callie Sue had told Papa all about Seth's visit, and his promise that he would return this morning to take Jeremy to the University Bible Class. Now they both looked questioningly at Papa, then at Jeremy who had made

no sign of moving from the table. Papa just shrugged his shoulders, shook his head, and finished his coffee.

All three were listening expectantly, and jumped and hurried to the door when they heard a clank and rattle and the sound of horses' hooves. Seth was coming down the road with his parents' surrey drawn by a pair of sleek horses. "Well, look there! It's Seth Bridges!" said Papa, trying to sound as if he had not been watching for just that person. "Wonder what he wants on a Sunday morning?"

Seth, dressed neatly in a dark gray suit, white shirt, and tie came briskly up onto the porch. Mama silently opened the door and glanced first at Jeremy, then back at Seth.

"Morning, Mrs. Cunningham. Morning, Mr. Cunningham. Callie Sue." Seth smiled and nodded to all. "Ready to go Jeremy? We're going in style! Dad let me use the surrey today!"

Seth saw that Jeremy still sat there dressed in his nightclothes.

"Well, I came a little early. Thought you might need a little help, seeing as how you haven't been going out much since you've been out of uniform."

He went over and touched Jeremy on the shoulder.

Angrily, Jeremy shrugged away the touch.

"I told you! I'm not going anywhere!" His words were wheezy and slurred, but there was no doubt about his meaning.

"Well, now, maybe you weren't quite sure what to wear to Bible class after wearing uniforms for so long. I think that suit you had for high school graduation ought to do just fine. That's what I've been wearing ever since I got back. Still fits pretty well, doesn't it?" Seth made a turn as though modeling his suit, then took a step toward the hallway. "I'll just help you find your shirt and get everything together."

CRASH!

Everyone jumped as Jeremy's hand hit the table, rattling the dishes, and spilling Mama's coffee. "You heard me!" he wheezed. "Don't act like you didn't! I'm not going anywhere!"

Seth turned slowly to Jeremy. He took a deep breath, glanced at Mama and Papa and then said quietly, "Yes, you are, Jeremy. I told you before. It's time you were getting back out and around. There are some people in Professor Smith's Bible class who have had just as hard a time as you have! You can't sit here feeling sorry for yourself the rest of your life. Now, I could always beat you in any wrestling match, and I guess I still can, even one-handed," he glanced at Papa, "especially if your Papa will help me."

While Papa hurried around the table, Seth removed his suit coat and carefully hung it over a chair. Then Seth took Jeremy by one arm, Papa took the other, and they carried Jeremy, struggling and swearing, down the hall. The door closed with a bang. There was the sound of scuffling, Jeremy's squeaky, shouting voice, then the coughing began. Still the door did not open.

Callie Sue looked fearfully at her mother who stood with one hand on the screen door, gazing at the overturned chair where Jeremy had sat.

"What should we do, Mama? What if Jeremy has a spell and can't breathe? Should we get the doctor?"

"No, Callie Sue, I don't think so. I think we should just wait. This may be an answer to my prayers," Mama said softly.

How strange to hear Mama talk about prayers! They hadn't been to church for so long. Not that anyone had said, "We won't go to church anymore." It had just kind of happened. Callie knew that she still talked to God, but hadn't realized that maybe Mama and Papa did, too.

Jeremy is loaded into the surrey against his will.

The bedroom door crashed open, and Seth and Papa brought out a red-faced, wheezing and struggling Jeremy. Jeremy was dressed, although not very neatly. He had lost so much weight that his high school graduation suit now hung loosely on his thin body. His shirt was sticking out of one side of his trousers, and his tie was somewhat crooked, but he was dressed!

    Seth stopped to straighten his own shirt and tie and replace his coat. Then he and Papa took Jeremy out to the surrey. With no help from Jeremy, they got him over the side and onto the seat. Papa placed the crutches beside him.

    "There'll be someone at the class to help him out of the surrey," said Seth as he turned the horses to drive off.

    Then Mama seemed to wake up. "Seth," she called, "can you stay for Sunday dinner when you come back?"

    "Sure," he called back, "then we can tell you all about the class!"

Chapter 6

"Mrs. Cunningham, I still say you make the best roast beef in the whole county!" said Seth as he added another slice to his already loaded plate. "Wouldn't you like another slice, Jeremy?"

Jeremy sat hunched over his plate as if no one had even spoken.

"Well, it sure seems like old times having you here! I just can't tell you how much we've missed you!" Mama looked fondly at Seth, then put her hand over her mouth. "Oh, my! I do hope your mother wasn't expecting you for dinner!"

"No, I told her I'd probably be eating here. You know, I must have eaten about half my meals here growing up, and the other half Jeremy ate at my house. So, I just figured I knew you folks well enough to know there'd be an invitation coming." Seth cleaned his plate with an amazing amount of one-handed skill. Callie watched, fascinated, thinking she would probably go hungry if she tried to eat with one hand behind her back.

"You've stayed away too long!" Papa said, as he wiped his mouth and put down his napkin. Mama brought the apple pie in from the kitchen and began to cut it. Mama, Papa, Callie Sue, and Seth had carried on a pleasant conversation about the weather and crops throughout the meal, but now they could not help looking expectantly at Seth. There was a silent question in the hot dining room air. What had happened during the two hours Seth and Jeremy had been away?

Seth stays for Sunday dinner

Seth first accepted a piece of the pie and then said, "That Professor Smith! I tell you he is really something! Don't you think so, Jeremy? Some people think he's a little crazy, struggling for something that seems so impossible. But others say he's already done the impossible more than once, and he sure has a way of inspiring a person! Why, when I'm sitting there in that Bible class, I'm convinced that if all of us just work as hard as he does and pray as hard as he does, we can do anything. Didn't you feel that way, Jeremy? Did you ever meet anyone like him?"

He looked questioningly at Jeremy. Jeremy looked up sullenly. "Crazy!" he wheezed.

Seth continued just as if Jeremy had agreed with him. "You see, Professor Smith got an idea right after he came here in 1914. He is an ordained Methodist minister, but he came here to teach sociology at the university. Well, right away, he decided that there needed to be a close connection between the Methodist Episcopal Church South and the university. He visited some universities where the church was working successfully with the students and came back with his mind made up that the best way was to build a church near the campus. It would coordinate church activities with university activities, but not be just a student church. It would still be a community church as well!"

"Oh, yes, I remember that," said Papa. "Created quite a stir as I recall."

"Yes," said Mama, "That was while you and Jeremy were still in high school, before you left for the--war." There was a little catch in her voice as if she could hardly say the word "war," but she continued. "We were in church every Sunday then, ourselves. No one listened to Professor Smith much at first. Then people began to look around, and realized that we were outgrowing our little church. We began to realize that we would have to move sometime."

With God's Help: Building the McFarlin Church

"But he still had a real battle trying to convince people that we needed a university church!" said Papa.

"Professor Smith has chosen what he thinks is the perfect spot for this church. If you stand on the steps of the university administration building and look straight north up University Boulevard, the street makes a little turn at Apache, so the lot stands out in plain sight. That's where we want to build this church! Two of the most important buildings in the students' lives looking straight up the boulevard at each other!" Seth seemed as pleased with the idea as if it were his own.

"I remember now," said Papa. "It was while Brother Welch was our minister in 1916 and 17. We knew that we were going to need to build a new church. I seem to recall that he agreed with Professor Smith on the site."

"Yes," said Mama excitedly. "I think it was in September of 1917 that the deal was closed on three lots at Professor Smith's choice of locations at University Boulevard and Apache. He and his students had collected lots of donations to cover the cost of the lots and the trustees agreed to buy them for the church."

"That's right," continued Papa. "Welch wanted to move right ahead with fundraising. Then, that fall, when Brother Walker was sent here to our church, Welch was appointed by the conference as pastor of the 'University Church,' even though it didn't exist yet. He even had an architect's drawing of how he hoped to build it. But the conference said it was not the time for a fund-raising campaign, with the war going on and so many other drives. I guess, too, the church members weren't quite ready for the University Church idea yet. Anyway, early in May of 1918, Brother Welch gave it up and moved to North Carolina."

"This was all going on before Jeremy and I went to the war. I can't believe we were just too concerned with getting graduated and enlisted to pay any attention to something so important. Do you remember knowing anything was going on, Jeremy?" Seth tried again to get some response.

"Bunch of nonsense!" muttered Jeremy in his squeaky voice, his eyes intent on his plate.

"Professor Smith kept quietly working away at his idea. But, when Brother Walker became our minister, he backed a different building plan. Walker's plan was to build a community church at the corner of Eufaula and Webster. Seemed like a pretty good idea, and something we might be able to do a lot sooner. The board voted to build there," Mama frowned and rubbed her forehead with the effort of remembering.

Professor Smith can still talk to groups about his idea, and if they want to give him donations for the University-Community Church project, he can accept them, but he can't start a campaign," said Seth. "Well, talk is just what he is doing. He talks about it every time he gets the chance. Some in his University Bible Class go with him and have learned his talk so well they can give it themselves. I've even gone with him some. Now we believe in this as

With God's Help: Building the McFarlin Church

much as he does. Most of us in the class have made pledges and are giving everything, we can toward the fund."

"There is a house on the lots we bought, and the class has been meeting there. The board named it the Guild House." Seth's voice showed obvious pride in the class and its accomplishments.

"But now," he sighed, "with the plans to build a community church on Eufaula Street, the Guild House will be used for a parsonage."

Callie Sue found the whole story of people she didn't know rather hard to follow, but she listened carefully, sensing how important it was.

"We're not giving up, though," said Seth. "We still believe in our University Church. We are still giving and collecting for our fund. Brother Smith and Brother Walker both want what they think is God's will for this community. Someday maybe they'll agree."

"It's an inspiring time to be involved," said Papa. "We're a part of building something that's going to influence people for years and years!"

"I miss going to Sunday School," said Callie Sue with a sigh.

"Maybe," said Papa, "Maybe, somehow, soon…"

Seth rose from the table.

"Time sure flies! I guess I'd better be getting on my way. Thanks again for the dinner Mrs. Cunningham. Jeremy, remember, I'll be here same time next week."

Jeremy had studiously ignored the whole conversation. Now as Seth moved out the door and down the steps, Callie Sue thought she heard Jeremy mutter something that sounded a lot like, "Don't bother!"

Chapter 7

All the next week, Callie Sue was busy helping her mother in the kitchen. It was July, and there were fruits and vegetables that must be canned or dried to put away for the winter. The two were at work by daylight boiling jars, peeling the peaches, or snapping the beans. The produce was placed in the sterile jars, covered with syrup or water and processed in the huge canner that sat on the kitchen stove. Callie's job was to scrub the jars and lids carefully before they were placed in the boiling water. She also helped snap beans and peel fruit.

It was hot, exhausting work, but by noon there would be rows of shining jars on the cabinet cooling. By evening they would be cool and ready to store in the cellar. Callie Sue was glad that they got up and started early so that they could be out of the steamy kitchen during the hottest part of the day. After dinner Callie had to stir the apples that were drying outside on the rack, then she was free to do as she wished until suppertime.

Most afternoons found her resting in the cool shade of the little cedar tree in the cemetery. Often Mr. Groggins came by and she helped him for a while, pulling weeds and grass away from the gravestones. On days when his arthritis was especially bad, Callie Sue helped as much as she could. They spent many hours working together and talking about the "old days" in Norman. Callie came to feel like she really knew Mrs. Groggins, the couple's three children, and ten grandchildren, just from listening to Mr. Groggins' stories about them. Somehow, though, she could never quite tell Mr. Groggins about her family, not with the way things were now. Mostly, she just listened as Mr. Groggins talked, and he never seemed to think it odd that a young girl spent so much time in the cemetery.

Callie Sue helps with the canning.

When Mr. Groggins wasn't around, she had long imaginary talks with little Robert McFarlin. She had no trouble at all telling him all that had happened. Whether she was talking with little Robert or listening to Mr. Groggins, her thoughts were never very far from the gloom and sorrow of the house across the road; Actually, harvest and canning time had made it seem not quite so bad. When they were so busy, Mama was almost like she used to be, giving orders and checking to see that Callie did everything just right. Papa brought big baskets of vegetables to the door for their attention. He always stayed close by to help when it came time to lift the heavy canner full of jars. Mama chatted and talked about how pretty the jars were looking. She even joked with Papa once that he wouldn't dare bring in one more basket of produce.

Soon, though, they heard Jeremy's door open and close, and Jeremy came shuffling down the hall to the table. Then Mama's face changed, and she stopped whatever she was doing to offer Jeremy breakfast. Most of the time he mumbled that he didn't want anything. Mama poured him a cup of coffee anyway and put the leftover biscuits on the table along with the butter and jelly. She and Callie then returned to their work, but the feeling had changed. Now, neither of them could forget the cloud that hung over their home.

Callie Sue also couldn't forget last Sunday morning, when Seth and Papa had made Jeremy get dressed and had put him in the surrey. She asked Mama early one morning while they were peeling apples if she hadn't been afraid the struggle would make Jeremy worse.

Mama paused in her peeling and gazed out the window thoughtfully. "Could it be any worse?" she said. "The doctor never said anything about needing to be careful what Jeremy does. For so long I kept thinking that surely, he would get better and be interested in some of the old things he used to do. But that just hasn't happened. So maybe it's time someone did something else. Jeremy and Seth always seemed closer than brothers. Maybe Seth can do something the rest of us can't."

Mama had never talked to Callie Sue that way before. Callie felt very grown up, hearing that confidence. She began to realize that no matter how hard it was for her, it was even harder for Mama and Papa.

Sunday morning came again. They were all at the table eating pancakes and bacon when, promptly at 8:30, Seth drove into the yard. They all glanced at each other, then at Jeremy, who sat there in his robe trying to ignore the sounds outside.

Seth came briskly into the house. "We're driving the buggy now," he said, gesturing at the door. "Mom and Dad are taking the surrey to church, and the buggy is plenty big for Jeremy and me."

The scenes from last week were repeated as Seth and Papa dressed a struggling Jeremy and loaded him into the buggy. They returned at noon, and again, Seth sat down to dinner with them. Later, when he drove away, promising to return next week at the same time, they all looked questioningly at each other, but no one said anything.

Next Sunday it happened again. After dinner Papa followed Seth out to the porch. Callie heard a bit of their conversation as Papa said something like, "Might as well give it up. We're not getting anywhere."

All she could hear from Seth as he drove away was, "Oh, No! We won't give up. I know this is the thing to do!"

Next Sunday, Mama, Papa, and Callie Sue sat at the table for breakfast.

"I just don't know," said Mama. "How long are we going to do this, forcing him to get dressed and go. It can't be doing him any good. He doesn't say a word, doesn't even talk to Seth. It's almost like he hasn't even been out of the house."

"I know," said Papa, "It doesn't seem to be doing him any good... but it's not making him any worse either! It's better to do something than just sit here and watch him ev..."

Papa stopped as they heard the bedroom door open and close. The clump and shuffle of crutches and footsteps came down the hallway. They all quickly put on cheerful, "Good Morning" expressions, hoping the subject of their conversation didn't still show on their faces.

Jeremy entered the dining room and moved toward his place at the table. Callie couldn't help herself. Her mouth dropped open, and she stared at him in surprise. Mama and Papa were staring, too.

Jeremy looked up at them as he struggled into his chair. "What's the matter?" he wheezed. "Didn't anyone ever see me dressed in my suit before? Did I get my tie crooked?"

He helped himself to a biscuit, buttered it, and began to eat.

Chapter 8

After Seth and Jeremy drove away, Callie stood on the porch with Mama and Papa, watching the dust clouds settle back onto the road.

"I really do miss going to Sunday School," she said. Papa stroked his chin thoughtfully.

"Well, there's no doubt the Lord knows where we are. He has surely heard our prayers whether we were here or at church. I do miss hearing a good rousing sermon now and then, though."

They looked at each other as if a new thought had just occurred to all of them.

"There's no reason at all for the three of us to sit at home every Sunday while Seth takes Jeremy to Bible class," said Mama. "I'll iron our Sunday dresses and brush Papa's suit, and we'll all go next week!"

All week-long Callie felt a happy anticipation that she hadn't felt since before Jeremy went off to the war. More than once she found herself under the little cedar in the cemetery telling baby Robert all about it.

"It's not that so much has really happened," she said, "but things seem changed a little anyway! Jeremy's still grumpy, but he seems different. He even told Mama, 'Thank you,' for baking his favorite dessert, a blackberry pie, the other day. Mama and Papa are different, too."

Callie frowned as she tried to sort out in her mind just what it was that had changed.

"Mama really smiled at me when she said, 'Good Morning,' today. She was even humming to herself while she ironed our Sunday dresses. It's like we all feel happier, but are afraid that, if we think about it, it might turn into a dream and go away!"

So, the week passed, with the heat at its fiercest as they neared the summer's end. Mama and Callie still worked daily with the canning. There was a sense of urgency as September drew near. Soon Callie would be going down the road to the little one-room school every day, and Mama would be left to finish the canning alone.

Early one morning they both had a surprise when Jeremy, dressed in overalls and a plaid shirt, came shuffling down the hall and asked if he could snap beans for them. Callie hurried to get him a basket of beans and a bowl as he sat at the table. She and Mama were barely able to contain their happiness, giving secret smiles to each other as they returned to work.

Sunday morning found Callie Sue and her parents having their breakfast early. Quickly Mama fixed a plate for Jeremy before she washed the dishes and Callie Sue dried.

Jeremy came to breakfast just as Papa went to hitch Beauty and Blaze to the buckboard, and Callie and Mama went to get dressed. He showed no surprise at finding his plate waiting on the back of the stove.

"I've kept your plate warm and poured your coffee, Jeremy," said Mama as she paused. "Hope you don't mind eating by yourself. We decided it was about time the whole family got back to church. We're all going today."

Jeremy just nodded and said, "Makes sense."

Seth arrived promptly and smiled approvingly when he saw the whole family dressed for church. As he and Jeremy climbed into the buggy, he said, "Mom's expecting Jeremy and me for dinner at our house today."

Jeremy looked up, surprised, but just raised his eyebrows and gave an almost unnoticeable nod of his head. Mama saw it though and smiled at Seth as if there were nothing unusual about the invitation.

Mama, Papa, and Callie sat in the buckboard and watched as Seth and Jeremy drove up the driveway and down the road. Papa waited until the dust had settled then he slapped the reins and started Beauty and Blaze up the drive. It wouldn't do to arrive at church all covered with dust.

There was a pleasant breeze blowing, and little puffy clouds drifted across the sky occasionally blotting out the sun. Callie looked up, drew a deep breath, and closed her eyes. She felt as if she would pop with happiness. Suddenly she had a strange thought.

"Mama," she said, "I think I'm praying! Not like Brother Walker used to in church or Mrs. Henderson in Sunday School, but my heart just keeps saying, 'Thank you, thank you,' over and over. Is that praying?"

Mama turned to look at her. "Yes, honey, it's the best kind."

The family returns to the First M.E. Church South.

"And that's a prayer I think we're all praying today," said Papa as he urged the horse along.

The morning passed in a haze of happiness. Mrs. Henderson hugged Callie Sue as she welcomed her to Sunday School class. Her friend Jenny came to sit beside her as if she had never been gone. Callie didn't even start to fidget while Mrs. Henderson taught the lesson. Could this be what it meant to grow up? Somehow, now, the Bible story and lesson seemed so much more important.

Later, in the little sanctuary, Seth and Jeremy slipped into a pew two rows back from Mama, Papa, and Callie. The singing in the little church had never sounded so beautiful.

"Praise Him, Praise Him" seemed to be just what was in Callie's heart. Brother Walker's sermon was "Blessings All Around Us," and Callie sat there thinking he must have written every word just for her.

Sunday dinner was a cheerful affair at the Cunningham's that day. Papa gave thanks to God for the food and for "... the way you remembered this family when we had forgotten you."

They chattered happily about how natural it seemed to have Jeremy gone to dinner with Seth's family, how happy people had been to see them back in church, and how Mama needed to pick out some of their freshly canned fruits and vegetables for the Missionary Aid Society to distribute to the poor. They sat for a long time at the table, just savoring the good feelings. Finally, Mama and Callie went to change clothes so they could clean up the dishes. Papa changed, too, and helped clear the table before going to stretch out in his easy chair to read the paper.

Mama and Callie Sue found themselves humming again all the songs they had sung in church that morning, and the washing and drying was done in no time.

Just as they were finishing, Seth drove his buggy into the yard. Jeremy climbed out slowly and carefully, but without any help. Seth turned the buggy around and waved as he left.

Jeremy clumped and shuffled up the steps and into the room with what seemed to be a real smile on his face. "Papa," he said, "could you give me some help? I need my old suitcase out of the attic. I'm going with Professor Smith on a trip this week."

Chapter 9

Monday morning Papa helped Jeremy get his suitcase down from the attic. Mama ironed an extra shirt for him. By Tuesday evening he was packed and ready to go. There was an unmistakable enthusiasm in Jeremy's voice as he told them the plan for the trip.

Jeremy, Seth, and Professor Smith would go by the Interurban to Oklahoma City on Wednesday afternoon, then on to El Reno. They would attend a prayer meeting that evening at the El Reno Methodist Episcopal Church South and talk with people about the need for the "University Community" church in Norman. If people asked to help, they would gladly accept their donations. They would stay in the home of a student whose parents lived in El Reno, and return to Norman by the Interurban on Thursday.

On Wednesday afternoon Mama, Papa, and Callie stood at the station watching Jeremy struggle aboard the Interurban car.

Callie wanted to stop Professor Smith and ask, "Are you sure you can take care of him? Maybe he really shouldn't go!"

Mama and Papa's faces told her that they were thinking the same thoughts. But, of course, you couldn't stop a grown man who has been to war and back. His family couldn't take care of him forever.

The family drives Jeremy to the Interurban in the buckboard.

How strange the house seemed when they returned home. They all tried to go about their usual chores, but found themselves pausing as thoughts of Jeremy crept in. "Of course," they reminded each other, "this is just what we've prayed for. He has to get out and be with people... do things!" Still the uninvited thoughts were there.

The evening seemed endless. Each of them wondered how Jeremy was managing in the home of a stranger this evening. Finally, the night passed and Thursday afternoon came. They climbed into the buckboard and rode to the station to meet the returning travelers.

With God's Help: Building the McFarlin Church

The electric Interurban car glided to a stop and the passengers quickly stepped down. Jeremy, Seth, and Professor Smith were the last ones off. There was no need to ask how the trip had been. There were smiles on all three faces.

Seth was full of enthusiasm.

"Professor Smith, I get more convinced about needing that church every time I hear you give your talk." He turned to the Cunninghams, "You should have heard him! Talking about how important it is to be able to coordinate students' religious lives and student lives! I don't see how anyone can help but be convinced!"

The professor looked proudly at the young men. Jeremy was nodding his agreement with Seth. Mama and Papa were looking carefully at Jeremy while trying to seem like they weren't. Their relief at seeing his interest and enthusiasm was obvious.

After all the greetings, Papa offered to take everybody home. There would be plenty of room in the buckboard. Soon they were loaded and on their way.

"How is the progress on the campaign, Professor Smith?" Papa asked as they rode along.

"Slow," said Professor Smith. "The pledges are coming in very slowly. Every little bit helps, but they add up so slowly. If we are going to build a church that will serve the university and the community for many years, there must be plenty of room for growth. That will take more money than the board is planning on."

"You don't think the building they're planning will be large enough?" asked Mama.

Professor Smith shook his head.

"If we were planning just for the community, or just for the university, or only for the next few years, yes, it would be fine. But, if we are going to plan for the future, for the way Norman and the university are going to continue to grow, we must think on a larger scale."

Speaking in a very serious voice, Seth said, "Not very many people agree with us, mainly because it's going to be nearly impossible to come up with that kind of money. They figure it's better to have a small building that will do for now, rather than to dream big for the future and wait."

"The people who believe in it don't have much money," wheezed Jeremy. "Even though many pledge, they don't add up to nearly enough."

"What we need," Professor Smith rubbed his chin thoughtfully, "is a few people who can make really big donations to move this campaign along. But I sure don't know where to find anyone like that."

They had arrived at the professor's home. He grabbed his suitcase and jumped out.

"Oh, well!" he said. "The Lord knows what He's doing. We'll mention it at our Bible class board meeting next Thursday. Jeremy and Seth, you both need to come and help me report on our successful trip. Many thanks for the ride, Mr. and Mrs. Cunningham."

He waved and went inside.

With God's Help: Building the McFarlin Church

Callie Sue sighed and settled happily back into her seat. It was so good to see Jeremy take an interest in something again! The cloud of gloom didn't seem to hang quite so closely over their house anymore. All the family had been so involved with their sadness that time had slipped by unnoticed. Now suddenly, it was almost autumn. Monday would be Labor Day, and then Callie would go off to school for a new school year.

"Mama," said Callie, "did you know that school starts next Tuesday? I need to get ready. I'm going to be in the fourth grade this year! Maybe Miss Miller will let me be a helper now, and when my work is done, I can help the little ones practice their reading or their addition facts."

Suddenly, Callie Sue found herself feeling excited as she looked forward to a new year. Things would continue to get better! She just knew it! Jeremy might never be the same as he used to be, but now he had a purpose and something to work for.

That night at the supper table Jeremy had some more surprises for the family.

"I've got to figure a way to earn some money of my own," he said. "I can't go around asking other people to pledge, unless I make a pledge first!"

Before the family could recover from their surprise, and while they were still trying to picture some job that Jeremy would be able to do with his one leg and weak lungs, Jeremy hit them with his next idea.

"Being with Professor Smith, thinking so much about the university's programs, and how they can coordinate with a university church--it has kind of started me thinking." Jeremy paused and looked around at his family. "I think there must be a way that I can go to the university! Half a leg and bad lungs haven't affected my mind any, and Professor Smith says that there will be some way to find the money for my tuition. Wasn't there an article in the paper a while back about veterans needing to fill out papers for disability pensions and bonuses?"

"Why, yes," answered Papa, "I think you're right. Seems like the people at the Red Cross were helping with all the paperwork. We can go down there tomorrow and check on it."

"Let's do that," said Jeremy. "I've wasted too much time already!" He paused and touched the stump of his leg experimentally. "And maybe... maybe it's time to see about that artificial leg. I hear the new ones work pretty well, and the end of my leg is not even tender anymore."

The family looked at each other with happy smiles. Their Jeremy was back!

He was full of plans and ambition again. Some of them might prove to be impossible, but they would make sure everything possible had been tried before giving up.

Chapter 10

On the Thursday after Labor Day, Callie Sue skipped along the road on her way home from school. As she came near the driveway she glanced across the road at the inviting coolness of the cemetery. On an impulse, she turned and went to the fence. It was early yet. It wouldn't hurt if she stopped for just a little while. She had come to this beautiful, peaceful place so often when she was sad, somehow it seemed only right that she should come here now when she could feel happiness and hope stirring in her heart again. She promised herself she would stay only a few minutes. She didn't want Mama to worry.

Callie tossed her bundle of books through the fence and crawled through after them. She picked up her books, and quickly sought out the shade of her favorite little cedar tree. She lay down in its shade and gazed up at the blue sky.

Callie let her mind drift over the last few days and the changed atmosphere in her home. Jeremy's conversation was full of deciding how he could earn a little money for his pledge. His possibilities were very limited, but he seemed confident that there was a way, and that he would find it. Then he had another surprise for them when he asked Papa if he could take the buggy and drive over to Seth's to talk about going to the University Bible Class board meeting Thursday night.

"If Seth can drive with one hand and one eye, surely I can do it with both hands, both eyes, and one good leg," Jeremy explained.

No one could deny that. So, Wednesday morning Papa helped Jeremy hitch Blaze to the buggy. Jeremy climbed in and drove a little hesitantly out of the yard. Two hours later he was back, beaming with pride and independence. On his own he had driven the three miles, and the plans for the trip to the board meeting had been made!

Then there was school! It was off to a good start. Callie had always been a good student, and Miss Miller was planning to let her help the smaller children who were having trouble with their lessons. Callie liked it so much, she thought she just might decide to become a teacher like Miss Miller when she grew up.

Her friends were as happy to see her as if she had been away. She realized now that she didn't remember much about the end of school last year. It was almost like she hadn't been there. Had all the sadness at home really affected her that much at school? Anyway, this was a new year, and she just knew it would be a good one!

Callie then became aware of a swishing sound nearby.

She looked over and there was Mr. Groggins, trimming the grass around one of the nearby gravestones.

"Well, Sis," he said, "haven't seen you much lately." "I know," said Callie Sue, "school started; but even before that, I just didn't seem to get over

With God's Help: Building the McFarlin Church

here much. I really should be home now. Mama will be looking for me. It just looked so cool and nice, I had to come for just a few minutes."

Mr. Groggins laid the scythe down on the grass, and rubbing his right hand, studied Callie carefully.

"I must say, you look a good bit different than when I first saw you over here."

"Everything's a lot different," said Callie Sue. "I guess I never really told you how terrible things were at home when Jeremy first came home from the war."

Mr. Groggins smiled understandingly.

"No, but I knew you felt like you were carrying the weight of the world."

"It'll never be like it was before," continued Callie, "but I don't mind being in the house now. Jeremy is interested, even excited, about building the new church. He's trying hard to find a way to earn some money so he can make a good pledge and maybe even go to the university. He is even talking about being fitted for an artificial leg! He's sure nicer to be around. I just hope he doesn't get discouraged trying to find something he can do."

Mr. Groggins went back to trimming the grass. "It sure is good to see you looking so much happier. Youngsters shouldn't have so much to worry about!"

"Well," said Callie, gathering up her books and brushing off her skirt, "I better get home and help Mama with supper. Jeremy is going with Seth to a meeting of the University Bible Class tonight.

He's driving our buggy all on his own! See you later, Mr. Groggins!"

Callie Sue and her parents are on the porch as Jeremy returns.

    Later that night, after the supper dishes were done and Jeremy had gone off proudly driving the buggy, Mama and Papa sat in the rocking chairs on the porch while Callie Sue sat on the steps and leaned back against the railing. Mama's hands were busy with her crochet hook and thread as she worked round and round a lacy white doily. The breeze was cool, and Callie sighed contentedly.

"Mama," she said, "do you think we'll ever get enough money to build that new church Professor Smith wants so much?"

"It may take an awfully long time, but as long as there are some determined people like Seth, Jeremy, and Professor Smith, it will get built," answered Mama.

"Do you think Jeremy's ever going to find some kind of job so he can earn some money for it?" Callie continued.

"Well," said Papa, "I sure hope he does. He should hear something before long on his disability pension. I do hope we manage to get something done on this church soon. I'd sure hate to see Jeremy get discouraged and lose his enthusiasm just when he's found it again. It does worry me some."

Just then, in the twilight, they could see Jeremy driving up the road from Seth's house. He pulled the reins to stop the horse by the porch.

"Wait till you hear what happened at our meeting!" Jeremy called hoarsely.

"I'll come help you put Blaze away," said Papa, getting up. "Then you can tell us all."

After the horse was cared for, Jeremy could hardly wait to tell his story.

"We were all getting discouraged about how slowly the money is coming in. We figure it will probably take years and years before we can start any kind of building."

"Just what we were talking about here," said Papa with a sigh.

With God's Help: Building the McFarlin Church

"We were all talking about how we need one really big donation. We were just sitting around thinking, and then Eugenia Messenger said, 'I know who our big donor could be!' When Professor Smith asked who she had in mind, she said, 'Robert McFarlin.'"

At that name, Callie sat up with her mouth open in surprise and said, "I know that name!"

Jeremy ignored her and went on with his story. "When Professor Smith asked why Mr. McFarlin should donate to our church, she told him that the McFarlins had lived here and been members of our church before they became rich in the oil business. Their little son had died while they were here. In fact, she said that he was buried in the cemetery just across the road. We all thought that Mr. McFarlin sounded like a good prospect, and agreed that we should ask Brother Walker to visit him and tell him about the church plans. Eugenia said that Mr. McFarlin is in poor health and is in a hospital in Baltimore, Maryland. So, our class will pay Brother Walker's expenses if he will go see Mr. McFarlin. Professor Smith is going to talk to Brother Walker tomorrow!"

"Robert Boger McFarlin," said Callie Sue, "aged 1 year 7 months and 10 days! That's it. I know that grave! Come with me in the morning before school, Jeremy, and I'll show you."

"The Lord works in strange and mysterious ways, more wonderful than we can imagine," said Papa, shaking his head in wonder.

As the family went into the house, they were filled with a feeling of awe at the way God was at work in their lives and in their community.

Chapter 11

As soon as breakfast was finished the next morning, Callie Sue dressed for school, grabbed her books, and she and Jeremy went across the road to the cemetery. Jeremy hurried as fast as he could, but Callie was already dancing with excitement beside the little cedar by the time Jeremy had shoved his crutches through the fence and crawled through after them.

"See," said Callie, "Robert Boger, Son of R. M. and I. M. McFarlin. That has to be Mr. Robert McFarlin." Jeremy bent down to study the stone carefully. "Must be," he said. "I sure would like to know some more about them."

"That was so long ago," said Callie. "I wonder if there is anyone still around here who remembers."

As they turned to go back to the fence, Mr. Groggins was coming up the path with his rake and tools.

"Morning, Mr. Groggins," said Callie Sue. "This is my brother Jeremy that I've told you about."

"Well," said Mr. Groggins as he offered his hand to Jeremy. "it's mighty good to meet you!"

Jeremy shook Mr. Groggins' hand and commented, "You're here awfully early. You must plan on doing a lot of work here today?"

Mr. Groggins shook his head. "Not really. I'm just kind of slow these days. My arthritis is getting

With God's Help: Building the McFarlin Church

so bad that I can't work long at a time. Most days I try to come early and spend a few hours before it gets hot." He looked around at the neat graves. "I don't really have to do all of them. Only a few families hire me, but I kind of like to see all the graves look nice. So, I just go ahead and trim all the ones that need it."

Jeremy looked around admiringly. "You certainly do a nice job." Then studying the stone again, he said, "We were just looking at this stone. If this means R. M. McFarlin, the oil man, he is a very wealthy man now."

"Yep! He's the same! Never would have expected it back in '95 when they moved away from here. They were just ordinary people. I remember it was awfully hard on them when the baby died. There were lots of children dying of typhoid fever then, but that didn't make it any easier. My memory's not too good, but Miranda, my wife, remembers. She and all the ladies in the church were kept busy trying to help the families where there had been deaths," said Mr. Groggins as he shook his head sadly and leaned on his rake, remembering.

"Do you think your wife might tell us about them?" asked Callie Sue. "I've kind of gotten to feel like they're good friends. I'd sure like to know some more about them." She looked up at the sun rising above the trees. "Oh, My! I'd better get to school or I'll be late."

"Well, Miranda loves company, and the only thing she loves more is having company come especially to hear her talk," said Mr. Groggins with a laugh. "Tomorrow is Saturday. Come over to the house in the morning and we can talk some more."

Callie Sue went off at a run through the fence and down the road. Jeremy thanked Mr. Groggins and shuffled away toward home.

Callie Sue and Jeremy visit Mr. and Mrs. Groggins.

Saturday morning found Callie and Jeremy along with Mr. and Mrs. Groggins sitting around the Groggins' kitchen with fresh hot cinnamon rolls and glasses of cool lemonade in front of them. Callie and Jeremy were eager to know more and begged Mrs. Groggins to get right to her story.

She searched her memory for a while, and began: "Yes, I remember the McFarlins. They were a fine family! They came here in about 1892. They had a daughter, Leta, and a baby boy, Robert. They were good church people, and came regularly to our Methodist Episcopal Church South. They lived in the 600 block on Main Street. Mr. McFarlin opened a feed store. He also bought and sold cattle. His feed store did very well, but the cattle business was pretty risky. It was a dry year, with very little grazing for the cattle. Then came the Panic of 1893. It all brought about an economic depression and he had to sell his cattle for less than he had paid for them. It seemed to take all his feed store profits just to cover the cattle losses.

"Then typhoid fever hit our community. If you've been over in the cemetery, I'm sure you've noticed how many young children died in 1893. Little Robert Boger McFarlin was one of them. Our church members did all we could to help. We sat with the family. We took food over. It seemed like none of us would ever get over missing that sweet baby. Those were hard times for lots of families, and the people who came here had to take care of each other and be strong.

Chapter 12

The Cunninghams rode quietly home in the buckboard on a cool Sunday in late October 1919. So much had happened that Callie Sue could hardly believe that only a few months had passed since Seth had first come to take Jeremy to church. The sun shone brightly, but there was no doubt that fall was in the air. The blackjack trees along the sides of the road were showing the promise of the red and orange foliage that they would soon wear.

Callie sniffed the air and thought that it had a different smell at this time of year, crisp and fresh. Blaze and Beauty still kicked up little puffs of dust as they trotted down the road in front of the buckboard, but the fall rains had begun and there were no longer the billowing dust clouds of summer.

The family was quiet as they rode along, each lost in thought about the services they had just attended. Jeremy had ridden home with them today, as Seth had stayed to help Professor Smith with some class business. It was only after they were inside the house that they noticed that Jeremy was especially quiet_ He went straight down the hall and into his room, shutting the door behind him. Mama and Papa looked at each other questioningly.

Callie watched them and fear became an aching pain inside her chest. Was it going to turn out that Jeremy's improvement was just a dream? Had they made a mistake by being too happy, and now it would all go away?

Quietly, Callie and Mama put the Sunday dinner on the table and called Papa.

"I'll get Jeremy," said Papa as he started down the hallway.

At the door he knocked and called, "Jeremy, dinner's ready. Better come quick before it gets cold."

From inside they heard, "Go ahead without me, I'm not hungry."

Papa turned to look at Mama and Callie, both standing nervously at the end of the hall. Then he turned resolutely back to the door, turned the knob, and went inside. "Now Jeremy, it's rude to your mother not to come to the table after she has prepared a good meal for us. If something has happened, it would be better if you tell us about it instead of trying to handle it alone."

There were muffled words from inside the room and again Papa's voice.

"We made some mistakes in this family until Seth showed us a better way! We're not going to make those mistakes again. Now, come on to dinner."

As they heard sounds coming down the hall, Callie and Mama hurried to sit at their places at the table, both trying to look as if everything were normal.

"I'm sorry, Mama," said Jeremy as he sat down, "I didn't want to upset the rest of you just because I was feeling discouraged."

As they ate dinner, Jeremy's story came out.

"We had such hopes for a good donation from Mr. McFarlin," he said. "You know Reverend Walker went to see him in the hospital in Baltimore. I guess the news is really not all bad. He didn't turn us down. In fact, he really wants to help us, but his company is involved in a big lawsuit and could lose a lot of money. So, he can't do anything until it's settled. That might take years."

"That doesn't sound so bad," said Mama "Our drive is no worse off than it was before, and we do still have a good hope for that big donation."

"I know," said Jeremy, "that's the same thing Professor Smith said. I guess it really wasn't right to let ourselves count so much on McFarlin, but we just couldn't help it. We felt like it was almost a sure thing, and we'd get this church started right away. Professor Smith said God has a plan in His own time, and maybe He's teaching us patience. I guess I just don't feel like learning patience right now."

Jeremy turned grumpily back to his plate and ate a bite of candied sweet potatoes.

"There's more, though," he said. "In a way, the possibility of a big donation makes it harder to go to others for the small contributions. A lot of folks might want to wait and see what happens. Then with Mr. McFarlin's health, he could die before his lawsuit is ever settled."

"We must pray for Mr. McFarlin," said Mama, "because he is a good man, not just so he can donate to our church."

With God's Help: Building the McFarlin Church

"That's still not all," said Jeremy. "When Brother Walker came to tell us about Mr. McFarlin, he also told us that the conference had transferred him to the church in Clinton. He and Professor Smith may not agree on everything about the new church, but we know how to work with him. A new minister is a whole new set of uncertainties."

"One thing we have learned in this family," said Papa shaking his head, "is that God still has a good supply of miracles left. We shouldn't make the mistake of thinking we need to do everything ourselves. We'll all just keep right on working away, making our own small contributions, and talking to everyone else about our campaign. He will work His miracles in His own time."

Callie felt tears coming to her eyes as she looked at Jeremy. "You just don't know how different it's been here since you started getting interested in building the church. If God made the change He's made in you, I know He will make the lawsuit come out right so the McFarlins can help. Please, Jeremy, don't go back to being sad and discouraged again!" She choked on the last words as she looked pleadingly at Jeremy.

"I'm sorry," said Jeremy, "I was awful to all of you when I first came back. I guess that, I of all people, should know better. You and Professor Smith are right. I have to keep right on working, putting in my own little bit. It will happen in God's time."

The family clasped hands around the table and bowed their heads, as Papa prayed, "Lord, teach us the patience to work diligently as we watch and wait for Your miracle. Amen."

    Callie added silently, "Dear God, is it selfish of us to ask for another miracle when you've already given us one? If it's not, and if you have another one to spare, we sure do need it!"

Chapter 13

Callie Sue sprawled on the grass by the little cedar tree in the cemetery. She rolled over on her back and looked at the tree. It wasn't very little anymore. It had grown until it was taller than Papa.

Callie had grown too. Here it was the fall of 1922 and Callie was now in the seventh grade at the little one room school. She loved and admired Miss Miller, and was sure that she wanted to be a teacher just like her. Even so, she also loved the free feeling of Saturday with no school. This Saturday had dawned unbelievably warm and sunny for the middle of November, and she had hurried through her chores so she could have some time outside.

There was nothing like fall in Oklahoma! It seemed like, overnight, the leaves had become gold, brown, and bright orange. The air was crisp and there was just a hint of smoke from leaves being burned. Callie rolled over again, savoring the crackle, crunch, and warm dusty aroma of the leaves that had fallen on the dry grass where she lay. "Why would anyone want to live anywhere else?"

Callie whispered to herself as she lay on her back studying the fluffy little clouds floating across the sky.

Tomorrow, after church, the family would celebrate Callie's twelfth birthday. Mama was cooking Callie's favorite dinner of baked ham and scalloped potatoes. There would be a beautiful three-layer birthday cake covered with mounds of fluffy white icing and sprinkled with sweet white coconut.

Jeremy shows his dad and Seth his artificial leg.

Callie's friend Jenny would be there and, of course, Seth. He seemed like part of the family again, almost like before the war. One Sunday Seth would have dinner with the Cunninghams, and the next, Jeremy would go to Seth's house. Papa had bought a new horse, Shadow, now that Jeremy was regularly driving the buggy. One week, Jeremy would drive Shadow pulling the Cunninghams' little buggy to get Seth and go to church, while the rest of the family went in the buckboard pulled by Blaze and Beauty. The next week Seth would come and pick up Jeremy.

Jeremy was now filled with plans and ambitions. He now had the full responsibility for the care of the cemetery. Mr. Groggins had started out having him do just a little trimming and weeding, waiting to see just how much Jeremy would be able to do. Jeremy had crawled along on his one good knee, dragging his crutches behind him.

Then, after many trips to Oklahoma City for fittings and therapy, Jeremy had finally come home walking on his artificial leg with only the help of a cane. He was awkward with the leg, and said it was not very comfortable. He was determined though, and with practice, he was getting more skillful. He could now walk along the paths with a hoe cutting away the grass and weeds without getting down on his knee.

Often on Saturdays, Callie Sue would go with him to help. She still had a bit of fear that he might get discouraged, give up the job, and go back to sulking in his room, but he didn't. In fact, he seemed to thrive on the work. His face was now tan and healthy looking. His voice was still wheezy, but he no longer seemed to worry about it. Other people understood him and they didn't seem to mind his voice, so he didn't either. He was helping Papa in little ways in the fields again. Jeremy often drove the team while Papa pitched in hay. He had also almost completely taken over the care of the vegetable garden.

Proudly, Jeremy put his whole $1.50 per week wages for the work at the cemetery into his pledge to the church building fund. When Mr. Groggins' arthritis became so bad that Jeremy was asked to take over the whole job, his pay went up to an unbelievable $3.00 a week! In addition, Jeremy had started to receive a small disability pension from the government. He now could pay his building pledge and even save some money.

Jeremy talked about enrolling in a full load of classes at the university. At Professor Smith's urging, he had enrolled in one class each semester all last year. His confidence had grown as he found that he could get himself to class and do the work just as well as any of the other students.

Callie often saw him studying the ads in The *Norman Transcript*. He would look longingly at the pictures of the sleek, shiny new automobiles. Then Jeremy would sigh and turn to the classifieds to see who might have a nice buggy for sale. There were sure to be some real bargains now that so many people were buying new automobiles.

The town of Norman was changing too. It was almost scary to go into town these days because of the automobiles that whizzed noisily by. The town marshals were enforcing strict speed limits, and even prominent city leaders had been fined for speeding. Still, Callie thought, you felt like you were going along at a snail's pace in a buggy or buckboard.

Papa often read the automobile ads too, and commented on how the prices were coming down. Soon motor cars would be within the reach of just

With God's Help: Building the McFarlin Church

about everybody. Mama would remind him then of the terrible stories they had read in the paper. People had been badly injured in collisions, and often cars had rolled backwards down hills when the drivers couldn't manage to shift into second gear without killing their engines. Sometimes the passengers had escaped, but at other times, there had been serious injuries or even deaths. Then again, just last week, they had seen Mr. Jenkins in church with a broken arm. He had broken it when the crank had flipped backward while he was trying to start his automobile. Mama didn't want any of her family in an automobile! It was just too dangerous!

Things were happening at the church too. Jeremy's discouragement at Reverend Walker's transfer had turned to hope when Reverend Broome arrived and his reputation became known. He was respected as a "builder" of churches, both in membership and buildings. By the summer of 1921, plans had changed again, and the trustees had voted to build on the lots at University Boulevard and Apache that had already been purchased with money raised by Professor Smith's class. Both the East and West Southern Methodist Conferences of Oklahoma had joined in the statewide fund drive, and plans were finally being drawn up for a university-community church. Funds were still accumulating very slowly though, and the starting date kept getting moved farther back. Still, Brother Broome remained confident that construction would start soon.

There had been a surprise at last week's annual conference meeting. The newspaper had reported that the Reverend Broome had been promoted to an important conference position as Secretary of Centenary Work. He was to immediately start his new job of collecting missionary funds statewide. The new minister, Reverend J. H. Ball, coming from Ada, would not arrive for another week, and there would be a guest minister speaking in tomorrow's service.

Callie sat up, shook the daydreams out of her head, and quickly finished pulling a few weeds from little Robert McFarlin's grave. She checked the other graves nearby, and pulled weeds from some of them. She stood for a while and watched as Jeremy worked on the other side of the cemetery. He was whistling softly as he worked his way along. Callie thought of how skillful he had become with the hoe and how he had even learned to push along a wheelbarrow loaded with his tools and cane. He covered more ground this way. Sometimes, when he did close work down on the ground, he removed the artificial leg and placed it in the wheelbarrow until he finished. He didn't even seem self-conscious about it anymore.

"Jeremy," called Callie Sue, 'Tm going on home to see if Mama needs me. I'll see you at supper."

Jeremy waved, and Callie hummed a cheerful tune as she crossed the road and went up the lane to the house. Somehow, she felt sure that her twelfth birthday, November 12, 1922, was going to be her best ever.

The next day the visiting minister preached a fine sermon on "Sharing Our Blessings." Callie Sue couldn't help fidgeting a little, thinking of the beautiful birthday cake waiting at home. She kept glancing across the church to where Jenny sat with her family. Jenny would ride with the Cunninghams after church and they would take her home after the birthday dinner.

Later, with church over, the girls chattered like two little sparrows during the ride home. Jenny teased Callie Sue by giving her just a glimpse of a small, brightly wrapped package hidden in the big pocket of her dress.

Jeremy and Seth would come along in the buggy later. Professor Smith had asked to see the members of the University Bible Class for a few minutes after the service. He must want someone to go on another fund-raising trip, the family thought.

The house was bright and cool. With the windows open, the breeze brought in the spicy scent of autumn. Callie Sue and Jenny helped Mama set the table and warm the food even though Mama laughingly protested that Callie was the "birthday girl" and Jenny was a guest. Just as they placed the last of the food on the table, they heard the buggy pull up out front.

When Jeremy and Seth came in, it was obvious that they could hardly contain their excitement. They managed to wait, however, until all were seated at the table, and Papa had given thanks for the food.

With God's Help: Building the McFarlin Church

"Do you want to hear some news?" asked Jeremy with a grin.

"From the looks of you, it must be good news," answered Mama.

"Well, it could be. The reason Professor Smith wanted to see us was to discuss some news he had," said Seth.

All eyes at the table were on the two young men who were agonizingly slow in telling their story.

"Reverend Ball will not be coming to our church," said Jeremy. "Instead, Reverend L. S. Barton will be coming from Boston Avenue Church in Tulsa."

"From Boston Avenue!" said Papa. "That's strange, he will be taking quite a cut in pay, and pastoring a much less prestigious church."

"I know," said Jeremy, "that's what we all thought." "There is unofficial word, though," continued Seth, "That he specifically requested the assignment, and ... "

He paused, looked at Jeremy with a smile, and they finished together, "... he has the support and approval of Mr. Robert McFarlin!"

There was silence around the table as they all thought through the implications of this news.

"The word is that Reverend Barton was the minister when the McFarlins lived in Tulsa and belonged to Boston Avenue Church. They also say that Mr. McFarlin has a great interest in the student religious work here in Norman," said Jeremy.

"What does that mean?" asked Mama.

With God's Help: Building the McFarlin Church

"Maybe nothing," said Papa, "but maybe a lot." "Why would he take a personal interest in appointing our minister unless he intends to become involved in building our church?" said Seth.

"This could be the way God is working out His plan! We will just have to wait and see," said Papa.

"Well," said Mama, "after news like that, my ham and scalloped potatoes can't compete, but they are getting cold. Is anyone hungry?"

Suddenly, they all were very hungry. They were feeling so thankful that Papa said another blessing, and they were soon enjoying the noisiest, happiest meal that that house had seen in many months.

After they had eaten the cake, Callie opened her presents. There was a beautiful white Bible from Mama and Papa, bright hair ribbons from Seth, a comb and brush set with mother-of-pearl handles from Jeremy, and Jenny's tiny package turned out to be a little cameo on a chain.

Callie Sue looked around the table happily. Her presents were all beautiful, but the news they had heard and the hope it had brought were the best birthday present she could imagine. She was sure she would never have another birthday to compare with today.

With God's Help: Building the McFarlin Church

Chapter 14

Papa drove the Cunninghams' buckboard down Main Street and turned south onto University Boulevard. Just a short distance from the hustle of Thursday afternoon traffic in downtown Norman, the road became narrow, with just enough room for a carriage or wagon. A wooden walk and bicycle path ran along beside the street. Soon they came to an intersection where many automobiles, carriages, surreys, buggies, buckboards, bicycles, and wagons were parked in an open field. People hurried across the intersection to the lot where many others were already gathered. A row of chairs had been set up and a few people, obviously honored guests, were sitting in them. Callie Sue and her parents joined the crowd, and looked curiously at the guests.

There was Reverend Barton who had come to their church last fall. Things happened quickly after that, leading up to today. By February, plans and contracts were prepared for starting the church. Then word had come from the McFarlins. They not only wanted to contribute to the church. They wanted to give the whole building and its furnishings in memory of their son! It would be a much larger church than anyone had dared to hope they could build. It was expected to cost $600,000. Just last week the trustees had accepted the McFarlins' offer. The new church would be called McFarlin Memorial

Methodist Church. Today, the ground-breaking ceremony would make it official.
"There are so many important guests here!" said Mama in awe.
"This is a great day for the Oklahoma Methodist Episcopal Church South. Now the work can really begin," said Papa. "April 5, 1923, will be a day to be remembered in Oklahoma! I imagine all the conference officials wanted to be here."
"Look," said Callie Sue, "there's Jeremy over there! Hi, Jeremy!"
She waved as she called out to him, then frowned as he didn't seem to notice her or his family.

In fact, Jeremy was very involved in conversation with an attractive young lady who stood near him. He seemed to be telling her something about the lots. She smiled, nodded, and looked where he pointed.

"Why, I believe that's Mary Jane Carpenter!" said Mama. "I haven't seen her in years, not since she and Jeremy graduated from high school. She surely has grown up. Her mother is in the Missionary Aid Society, and I believe she said Mary Jane has started classes at the University."

"Well, I declare! What do you suppose that's all about?" said Papa as he grinned, raised an eyebrow, and winked at Mama.

Just then, Reverend Barton came forward. He beckoned for everyone to gather round, and give him their attention. An expectant hush fell over the crowd as he called on their former minister, Brother Broome, to lead the prayer. Then, Brother Barton made a few remarks similar to the thoughts Papa had expressed about the importance of the day for the Methodist Episcopal Church South, and for Norman. Then Reverend Barton turned, looked along the row of dignitaries, and made a joke about it being the most dressed up crowd he'd ever seen come out to wield shovels. After the appreciative laughter died away, he started the introductions of the guests.

    First, just as Papa had predicted, he introduced officials. There were so many that Callie gave up on trying to remember them all. She just knew they were all very important. There were speeches from some of the guests. They spoke of the responsibility that such a gift placed on the Southern Methodists of Norman. There were congratulations on having among their membership those who were such good stewards of their gifts.

    Finally, all the guests had been introduced, except a dignified gentleman and a pretty, grandmotherly lady seated next to him. When Brother Broome introduced Mrs. Robert McFarlin, the applause and the cheers were deafening. The crowd was saddened to hear that Mr. McFarlin was too ill to be there. The gentleman with Mrs. McFarlin was John Rogers, their lawyer and representative.

    Callie didn't hear or understand much of what was said after that. She was standing on tiptoe, concentrating on trying to get a good look at Mrs. McFarlin.

    "Callie, don't stretch and crane your neck around like a rooster! At twelve years old you need

to try to act a little bit like a young lady," said Mama reprovingly.
Callie noticed, though, that Mama was smiling and kept moving around to get a better look at Mrs. McFarlin herself.
Finally, all the guests, including Mrs. McFarlin, left their chairs to gather around as Mr. T. E. Smith, president of the church board of trustees, and Mr. Robert Bell, president of the University Student Council, picked up two shiny new spades. They each turned a spade of dirt and then placed the dirt in a special metal container, which Brother Barton explained was to be put in the cornerstone of the new building.
A cheer went up from the crowd, and Callie Sue was sure that it was heard all the way back to Main Street. Work had officially started on the McFarlin Memorial Methodist Church!
Callie Sue was excused from school for the afternoon. Miss Miller had given permission for students to miss the afternoon's school for the ground breaking on the condition that each student would write an essay describing the day and its significance. The assignment changed the minds of a few who thought it might be an easy way to get out of half a day's school!
Callie, though, could hardly wait to get started on her essay. The ride home seemed longer than ever before. There was so much to tell! She was afraid she might forget some details if she didn't start writing it soon.

With God's Help: Building the McFarlin Church

As soon as they were home, Callie grabbed a pencil and writing tablet. As she hurried for the door, she turned back to the hallway.

"Mama," she called, "is it all right if I go over to the cemetery for a little while? I'll be back to help with supper."

Mama agreed, with warnings to be careful of her good clothes, and a few minutes later, Callie was sitting comfortably in the shade of the cedar tree in the cemetery. Her pencil flew across the pages of her tablet as she described the wonderful events of the afternoon. Now and then she would stop to chew on her pencil and think. Then she would write on, faster than before.

She was so absorbed in her work that she didn't notice when a quiet, sleek automobile glided to a stop along the cemetery lane. She also didn't notice the driver who held open the car door or even the woman who got out until she had walked across the grass and stopped just a few feet from Callie.

Startled, Callie Sue dropped her pencil and looked up. She gasped in surprise as she gazed into the face of the pretty, grandmotherly lady.

Of course! She should have known Mrs. McFarlin would come here! It was her son Robert's grave! And here she had come and found Callie Sue sitting on it!

With God's Help: Building the McFarlin Church

Callie and Mrs. McFarlin meet at the grave.

"Oh, I'm sorry," said Callie, gathering her books and papers. "I'll get out of your way!"

"Don't hurry," said Mrs. McFarlin, "you look so comfortable."

Mrs. McFarlin looked around her. "Oh! The place has become beautiful! It was just an open field when we buried him here! In fact, it's so beautiful now, I think I would come here, too, if I needed some quiet to do my lessons." Mrs. McFarlin turned back to smile at Callie Sue, and then knelt down to look at the stone.

"It has been kept so beautifully," she said. "Not a speck of dirt or a bit of grass on it!" Mrs.

With God's Help: Building the McFarlin Church

McFarlin caressed the stone with her fingers and traced the letters.

Callie quietly turned and started to leave.

"Wait! Don't go!" called Mrs. McFarlin. "Come, tell me about yourself. Do you come here often?"

Soon, without really knowing how it had happened, Callie found that she had told this gentle lady all that had happened since Jeremy had gone away to war. She didn't know why she was telling all this to a stranger, but it just seemed natural. Perhaps it was because she had come here and visited little Robert so often through that difficult time!

Callie glanced up at the sun as it was sinking lower in the western sky.

"Oh my, I better go. Mama will think I'm lost." Mrs. McFarlin took her hand and said sincerely, "Callie Sue, I am very pleased to have met you. Thank you for sharing your story with me!"

"I'm sorry that your little boy died all those years ago. It must have been terrible for you," said Callie, "but I am so happy you are building this church. It is important to so many people. Your little boy will surely be remembered! Bye now!"

Callie dashed for the fence, crawled through, and ran home. She wondered how she could wait until after supper and washing dishes to get back to her writing. Her mind reeled with ideas. What a finish she had for her essay now!

With God's Help: Building the McFarlin Church

Chapter 15

Spring of 1923 turned into summer with dependable regularity. The students said good-bye to Miss Miller and each other for the summer and departed for their usual hot-weather activities. All had obligations to help with the farm chores around their homes. The boys would spend a good part of their summer in the fields driving their fathers' teams, helping to plant the crops, or chopping weeds away from the precious tender shoots of cotton or com. The girls, like Callie, would find much of their time was needed to help in the kitchen.

At twelve years old, Callie Sue was expected to take a large share of the responsibility for chores now that she was home from school. Often, she spent the morning helping in the vegetable garden. Then the laundry had to be done each Monday. Most families in town now had electricity and electric washing machines, but the electric power lines had not come out to their farm yet, so they still used their kerosene lamps and did much of their work as they had always done it. They had bought a washing machine, and it was a great help_ Still, she or Mama had to stand and turn the handle to move the wooden paddle that swished the dirty clothes through the soapy water until they were clean. Then one person would turn a handle while the other fed the wet clothes through the soft rubber rolls of the wringer into the rinse water. If it was this much work now, Callie wondered how they had ever had clean clothes before they got the washer!

Of course, there was still the canning and drying of fruits and vegetables, as well as the house cleaning. Now Callie did much more than just wash the canning jars and stir the drying fruit.

What Callie really liked, though, was to go outside. Often, she put on a straw hat to shade her face from the sun and rode out to the field with Papa to spend the morning cutting weeds, or planting seeds, or helping with whatever he was doing that day.

Growing up wasn't just work, though. There were things to do now that one couldn't do at eleven years old! There was, Epworth League at the church each Sunday evening. Papa or Jenny's father would take Callie Sue and Jenny to town to the meetings. Then, sometimes, during the week Mr. and Mrs. Johnson, who taught the junior girls' Epworth League, would take them on an evening picnic or even to spend an afternoon at the bathing pool at Doll's Park.

Jeremy now had his own buggy and drove Papa's horse, Shadow. He was usually glad to drive Callie Sue and Jenny into town to meet with the group to enjoy a glorious afternoon in the cool water with their friends.

At these times, Jeremy stayed in town instead of going home while the girls were at the party. He would drive out to the church site at University and

With God's Help: Building the McFarlin Church

Apache, park his buggy in the shade, and watch whatever activity might be going on that day.

At first there was very little. He came home frustrated and said, "How are we ever going to have that new church if they don't get started? I don't think they have turned another shovel full of dirt since the ground breaking."

As the summer wore on, however, things began to happen. A gigantic hole appeared in the middle of the lot as the excavation for the basement started. Now it seemed as if Jeremy couldn't spend enough time there.

Callie shared his excitement, as did others. Often Jeremy would drive to the university campus to pick up Mary Jane Carpenter after she finished her summer classes for the day. Then they picked up Callie Sue, and the three of them went to check on the latest developments at the building site.

Summer became fall, and Callie could not believe that she was starting eighth grade, her final year at the little school she had attended for the past seven years. Next year she would be going into town each day to the high school!

Jeremy's friend, Seth, had decided to take the plunge this year and was a full-time student at the university. Professor Smith had talked seriously to both Seth and Jeremy about university degrees ever since they first began attending the University Bible Class. Both Seth and Jeremy had taken a few courses. Now, Seth had some long, serious talks with Reverend Barton about the best courses for him to take if he wanted to go to seminary and become a minister. The Cunninghams, his family, and his friends encouraged him and assured him he would be an excellent minister.

Callie and her family could see that Jeremy felt quite restless. Even though Professor Smith told him he should start full time classes at the university, Jeremy was still hesitant. In spite of his success in the classes he had taken and his physical improvements, he held back on any decision. For the fall semester he had again enrolled in only one course. As the weather became cooler, Papa needed less of Jeremy's help, the work at the cemetery took less time, and he found himself with hours of free time. More and more of these hours were spent in Norman at the building site. Jeremy came home each evening and related to the family the progress that day. He talked about the size of the basement being prepared, the enormity of the stones being shipped into the site, and the cranes, ropes, and pulleys used to move the materials around. Most of all he was impressed by the architects and supervisors' reading and interpretation of the plans as the structure took shape.

Workers at the site became quite familiar with him. When he took Callie Sue to the building site one afternoon, she was surprised to hear the supervisor call Jeremy by name and give him a friendly wave. Jeremy parked the buggy, and they got out and walked over.

Jeremy steadied himself with his cane as he confidently led her around. As he had spent more time in work and exercise, his walking had now become so smooth that people hardly seemed aware of his artificial leg.

Jeremy and Mary Jane visit the construciton site.

"Are you sure we should be over here?" Callie Sue asked.

"Oh, sure," said Jeremy, "I come all the time."

He then took her all around the site. Callie Sue worried that any minute someone would tell them to get off the site and out of the way. It was obvious, though, that he knew how to find his way around without interfering with the actual construction work.

No one told them to leave. In fact, the workers paused to talk with Jeremy and to explain to Callie what they were doing. One man showed her the number on a huge stone block, and explained that it indicated where it would go in the finished building. Jeremy then showed her where the tall steps would lead up to the sanctuary. Callie couldn't believe how much Jeremy knew about the building just from his long hours of observation.

Summer and fall passed. As winter approached, Jeremy brought home more catalogs from the university. Callie frequently saw him frowning over his personal account book, adding and subtracting figures.

Finally, Callie overheard him talking with Mama and Papa. He had saved enough from his pension and the work at the cemetery for his tuition and books. If Papa could get along without his help on the farm, Jeremy wanted to start full-time classes at the university next September.

In the midst of Jeremy's struggle with his decision came an important development at the building site. January 21, 1924, was the date set for laying the cornerstone. The day was windy and the cold was penetrating, the whole Cunningham family was there to watch, along with many other members, and church and city officials.

The items to go inside the cornerstone had been carefully chosen. There was a Bible and a copy of The Discipline of the Methodist Episcopal Church South. Of course, these represented the whole reason for having a church! Current copies of The Norman

With God's Help: Building the McFarlin Church

Transcript would show what was happening in the community, and the impact this church would have on it. There was a copper plate inscribed by the contractor with some information about the building. Then, Reverend Barton asked if anyone wished to place anything else in the cornerstone. To everyone's surprise, Mr. L. L. Logan, Sunday School Superintendent, came forward and presented some treasured mementos from the Holy Land. He explained that the dried leaves were from the Garden of Gethsemane, the dried Olives from the Mount of Olives, and the small stone was from the village of Nazareth. He received a hearty "Amen" from the crowd when he said that these items would forever attest to the bond between this church and its Christian beginnings in the Holy Land.

Callie shivered inside her warm coat and watched with interest as the items were placed inside a copper box, and then inside the cornerstone. Mr. and Mrs. McFarlin and one of their daughters, Mrs. Walters, were there to help seal the stone. Callie felt thankful that Mr. McFarlin was well enough to come. Callie Sue caught Mrs. McFarlin's eye and saw a smile of recognition. When Mrs. McFarlin said something to her husband, he looked and smiled, also.

When the ceremony was over, Callie Sue closed her eyes and tried to imagine in place of the machinery and piles of stone, the magnificent structure that was to stand on this corner.

"How can we ever wait? It seems like it takes so long!" said Callie to Mama and Papa.

"We've lived through a lot of waiting already and we managed," said Mama with a smile.

Papa looked around at all the stones and equipment. "We know that God is working out His plan on this corner. We may not understand His timing, but we know it's right. We can wait!"

Chapter 16

Callie Sue followed Mama and Papa down the sloping aisle and into a pew near the center of the huge new sanctuary. She ran her hand over the satiny smooth dark walnut finish and appreciatively sniffed the new wood smell in the air. She tipped her head back to see the ceiling far above the gathering congregation. After attending so many services in the old, small sanctuary, Callie Sue felt almost as if she were outside looking up at the sky.

She looked at the front of her bulletin and read, "McFarlin Memorial Methodist Church." Inside she read, "Sunday, December the 7th, 1924, Morning Services." Just as if there were nothing unusual about today!

Muted sunlight streamed through the pale green and gold tapestry glass of the windows and was reflected from the shining carved wood all around them. Callie turned to gaze at the balcony that curved around the sides and back of the sanctuary. At the front of the room, the altar rail, the pulpit, and the choir screen were carved in beautiful arches and scrolls and glowed with the same dark finish as the pews. Above the choir loft gleaming gold-colored pipes covered the wall, and behind the organ screen more pipes could be glimpsed. In front of the screen sat the organ console where the

With God's Help: Building the McFarlin Church

organist would soon bring forth music such as most of the congregation had never heard before.

Again, Callie Sue tipped her head far back and studied the chandeliers. There were ten of them suspended by chains from the high ceiling. The glass shades were lightly tinted so that the light from them was soft yet clear. As she studied them, Callie discovered that the metal parts had been colored lightly to blend with the woodwork.

At fourteen years Callie was still the official "duster" at home and couldn't keep the stray thought from her mind, "I wonder how they will ever get up there to dust them!" Callie smiled and shook the incongruous thought from her head.

Callie had been so absorbed in looking at everything,

she had hardly been aware of others coming in to sit around them. The huge room was nearly filled. Everyone in Norman and for miles around must have come for this special service, thought Callie. Even though the sanctuary was almost filled, there was an unusual quietness in the air. All those present gazed in quiet awe at the wonders of this new building. She saw the members of the University Bible Class come in and fill several rows at the front of the balcony. She smiled and nudged Mama when she saw that Jeremy was sitting next to Mary Jane Carpenter.

Already this morning there had been Sunday School for all ages. Classes had met for the first time in the spacious rooms filled with glowing new furnishings. Somehow the lesson had seemed more

With God's Help: Building the McFarlin Church

meaningful than ever before as they sang praises, gave thanks, and studied the old, old stories.

Callie Sue couldn't help but jump with surprise as the first notes from the organ filled the huge space. All around them people sat enthralled as the air fairly vibrated with the glorious music. When the prelude was over, Callie realized she had scarcely breathed for fear of missing a note. She drew a deep breath and stood with the congregation to sing. The choir entered as everyone joyfully joined in singing "Holy, Holy, Holy." The long-awaited service of dedication began.

Callie Sue was quite a grown-up young lady now, but not so much so that she didn't sometimes get restless and let her mind wander when the church services seemed extra-long. Today was a different matter! She felt as if she were hanging on every word. How she wished she had some paper and could write fast enough to write it all down to relive it weeks and months later! Instead, she just tried to memorize everything that was said or done.

Brother Barton came forward and read the scripture from a large new Bible on the pulpit. Callie thought that the choir must have practiced for months on the anthem, "The Heavens Are Telling." She closed her eyes and imagined that this must be what a choir of angels sounded like.

When it had been announced that Bishop Mouzon would preach the sermon and conduct the dedication, Papa had explained to Callie Sue how the Methodist Episcopal Church South was organized into East and West Conferences in Oklahoma. He explained that Bishop Mouzon was a high official in the church, and was in charge of all the Methodist Episcopal South churches in the West Conference. Now, as Bishop Mouzon preached, he talked about how McFarlin Memorial Methodist Church would serve as a living memorial to the child who had died, and to the love and kindness shown by the community. It was an especially appropriate memorial because it would serve both the young people at the university and the families of the community. Callie Sue sat thinking about how much the church had done for her family even before it was built! The Cunninghams could now look forward to the future that Bishop Mouzon was talking about.

There were so many visiting ministers at the dedication ceremony that Callie Sue couldn't begin to remember all their names. The people she did know, however, were Robert and Ida McFarlin. When they stood and came forward, Callie wasn't sure, but she thought Mrs. McFarlin caught her eye and gave her a special smile.

With the simple words, "We present this House to the future worship of God," the ceremony was finished.

As the Cunninghams left the sanctuary, they paused to read the plaque that read: "The McFarlin Memorial Methodist Church was erected in the years of our Lord, Nineteen Hundred Twenty-three and Nineteen Hundred Twenty-four, to the glory of Almighty God, with prayers that His Spirit may dwell here, by Robert M. McFarlin and his wife Ida

With God's Help: Building the McFarlin Church

Barnard McFarlin in memory of their little son Robert B. McFarlin whose dust now reposes in the cemetery one mile North of this Church. This House of Worship is built for the Youth of Oklahoma and the People of Norman, and whomever may find it in their hearts to hear."

The Cunninghams listen to the chimes with Seth and Mary Jane

"Isn't it wonderful," said Callie to her parents, "there was so much sadness, but it resulted in all this today!"

With God's Help: Building the McFarlin Church

"Don't underestimate the guiding hand of God," said Papa. "Sometimes we forget that God is in charge, and He knows what He is doing!"

Jeremy caught up with them just then, wheezing and breathless, but smiling.

"Is it all right if Mary Jane and Seth both come to dinner with us?" he asked.

Of course, Mama approved. What a parade they made! Callie Sue went with Mama and Papa in the buckboard, Mary Jane and Jeremy were next in his buggy, and finally Seth followed in his own buggy. Eagerly, they started the drive home, where dinner had been left slowly cooking.

Dinner was a festive affair as they relived the exciting events of the dedication. Last evening, they had all attended a reception for the special guests. They had been amazed at how the McFarlins seemed to be just ordinary people like themselves.

"I would be willing to take a few million dollars just to find out if I could stay that nice," mused Jeremy, and everyone laughed with him.

At the reception, Mrs. McFarlin had recognized Callie Sue. She introduced Callie to Mr. McFarlin who asked if she still visited her cedar tree near their son's grave. Callie Sue assured them that she did, and that she had pulled the dry grass away from the stone just that morning in preparation for the special day.

They relived the wonders of the morning service with all agreeing that it couldn't have been more inspiring and meaningful. They all planned to return to church in the afternoon when Mr. Noll, the organist, would give a concert and another guest minister would speak. They would take a basket along, filled with leftover snacks so they could stay on for the evening service. By staying, they would be in town to hear the playing of the chimes in the tower far above the street calling worshippers to the service and to the first Sacrament of Holy Communion in the new church.

There was a lull in the conversation as they contemplated the satisfaction of a delicious meal, an inspiring morning, and the anticipation of an equally inspiring evening. Jeremy glanced nervously at Mary Jane and started to speak. He found his voice unusually squeaky, cleared his throat, and tried again.

"Mary Jane and I have made some plans we think you should know about," he said.

Mama and Papa smiled at each other, and Mama seemed to have a twinkle in her eye as she asked, "Oh? What could that be?"

"Well, even though I started going full time to the university in September, you know I hadn't really decided what degree I wanted. Finally, now, I know. I guess I have really known ever since they started building on the church. I just can't describe how I've felt watching it go up. I want to take architectural engineering. I want to be able to build something as magnificent as that!" Jeremy explained. "It will take a long time, and lots of work, but I know now that I can do it. My veteran's disability money and my work at the cemetery are covering the cost with a little left to save."

With God's Help: Building the McFarlin Church

He reached over and took Mary Jane's hand. "Mary Jane and I have decided that we want to marry." Then he added quickly, "Not right away, though. We will just be engaged for a while. Mary Jane is finishing her degree this year, and will take a job teaching while I am still in school."

Although the announcement was not a complete surprise, no one had expected it just now. They all jumped up and hurried around the table to hug the beaming pair.

Later, when some of the excitement was over, the dishes were done, and it was not quite time to go back to town, Callie Sue took Mama aside and said, "Mama, I won't be long, but I really want to go over to the cemetery for a little while."

Mama smiled and nodded with understanding.

"Of course, it's all right. We have about thirty minutes before we need to go."

The grass of the cemetery was dry and brown in the chilly December sunlight. The dark green of the cedars gave such softness and color that the place was still beautiful and peaceful even in the winter. Callie Sue went straight to her cedar and sat on the dry, prickly grass next to it. As she sat there, she thought about all the events of the five years since she had first come here. Her heart was so full of thankfulness she felt she could hardly breathe.

A little self-consciously at first, then confidently, she got to her knees and folded her hands.

"Oh God," she prayed, "how can you have time to take care of all the world, and still look down and give such special attention to me and my family? You have brought together so many wonderful people to make things happen. Thank you for all our friends, Seth, Mary Jane, and all the people at church. And dear God, thank you for Professor Smith, all our ministers, and most of all for Mr. and Mrs. McFarlin. In bringing them all together to build a church, you have also rebuilt my family. I should have known that You had a plan for us. Lord, let me always remember!"

    Callie Sue got to her feet, brushed the grass from her knees, and started across the road in joyous anticipation of the rest of the day's activities, and of the years to come.

The End

From the author

I hope that you have enjoyed this visit to McFarlin's beginnings.

Thank you for reading
Beverly Sanders

Other Works by
Beverly I. Sanders

Into the Unknown, Book 1: Journey in Faith Series
Published in 2019
Guest for Unity, Book 2: Journey in Faith Series
Published in 2023

Made in the USA
Monee, IL
29 January 2024